So i

She felt the tug of unused muscles in her calves and stopped to catch her breath. There was a time when this had been a daily walk, a daily pleasure. Somewhere here on the left had been the old Mensa where they had eaten cheap, awful food for lunch and just beyond it the cafe where they paid more than the price of lunch for a cup of coffee and a piece of rich cake.

The bookstore. In the window a set of old books, perhaps a first edition. As a student she had not been able to afford such luxuries. She could buy it now, but what would she buy?

She turned away from the window. Walking briskly now, she passed through the empty marketplace and found a little cobblestone street that slanted upward.

Now the whole town lay below her, hundreds of red roofs, the river in the distance.

Down below, if she kept the angle of her vision narrow, she would see only the old, the memorable, the beloved. From this vantage point, it might be twenty years ago or more.

She let the tears come. They were long overdue . . .

LET PINNACLE BOOKS
LEAD YOU TO THE
SUMMIT OF ROMANCE

LOVE'S AVENGING HEART   ($3.95, 17-302)
By Patricia Matthews
Beautiful Hanah thought only of escaping from her brutal stepfather, Silas Quint. When he sells her into servitude as an innkeeper's barmaid, Hanah faces the toughest battle of her young life. The fiery redhead faces cruelty and humiliation as she struggles for her freedom and searches for a man to fulfill her dreams.

LOVE, FOREVER MORE   ($3.95, 17-244)
By Patricia Matthews
When young Serena Foster's parents were suddenly killed, she found one night's comfort in arms of young Rory Clendenning. But one night of passion cannot last forever, and when rugged Darrel Quick came into her life, Serena discovered a new and very different type of love. Serena finds a new vision of her destiny as a woman as she searches for *LOVE, FOREVER MORE*.

SWITCHBACK   ($3.95, 17-136)
By Robin Stevenson and Tom Blade
When Elizabeth took her grandmother to a silent film retrospective, she never could have imagined the events to come. Dorothea saw herself in a movie starring the love of her life, Vernon Dunbar, yet she could not remember it all. If only Elizabeth could travel back in time and sort out her grandmother's secretive past . . .

ONLY
YESTERDAY

SYRELL
ROGOVIN
LEAHY

PINNACLE BOOKS
WINDSOR PUBLISHING CORP.

In memory of Ingrid

PINNACLE BOOKS

are published by

Windsor Publishing Corp.
475 Park Avenue South
New York, NY 10016

First Pinnacle Books printing: October, 1990

Printed in the United States of America

Part One

Chance cannot change my love, nor time impair.
"Any Wife to Any Husband"
—Robert Browning

Chapter One

The American woman got out of the taxi and walked across the still-soggy ground to where the members of the family were clustered at the gravesite. Even with only their backs visible, they were easily distinguishable: the strong, firm, slender figure of the mother, her hair, as always, in place; the older daughter, Marie-Luise, to her mother's left; the younger, Martina, to her mother's right; their respective husbands; three children in three distinct sizes. In the space between the skirts of their coats, the bright white of a gravestone was partly visible. The American woman had seen it only once, when she had visited a few months after the death of the father. That had been the first painful visit; he had figured so warmly and so profoundly in her life.

She was close enough now to hear the small sounds of grief as her shoes made their own squishy sounds on the rain-soaked earth. Nearing the group rekindled emotional fires she had tried to quell for hours on the plane and on the long ride that followed. Returning to this country, to this town, to these people, was ordinarily a journey of joy, but if she lived another forty-two years, she would not experience such feelings of sorrow as those that overcame her now.

The figure to the left of the mother turned at her approach and an almost smile lighted Marie-Luise's clear, beautiful face, after twenty years still the same face that had greeted her on the railroad platform that rainy fall evening at the start of her year abroad. Marlies leaned toward her mother and whispered something, then left the group, her arms opening as she moved.

"Lee. Thank you for coming," in that wonderfully clear German that had made the first days much easier.

"I came too late," and the sadness overflowed in tears.

"No, you're not too late. When she was still awake, we told her you were coming and she smiled."

A smile for the American woman who had flitted in and out of the girl's life for all of her nineteen years, a big sister, a distant cousin, a friend from abroad brimming with love and gifts.

The whole family turned away from the grave. The mother, her face stained with tears and her eyes worn with weeping, nodded at Lee. They embraced and the mother said, "It's over."

"Yes." She remained facing the open grave, holding Frau Biehl's arm, as much to steady herself as to steady the older woman.

Marie-Luise brought the priest over and Frau Biehl said, "This is our American friend, Mrs. Linden." She used the word "Mrs." when she spoke German, as Lee

8

always referred to her as Frau Biehl when she spoke English.

The priest mumbled something and Lee shook his hand. In front of her the casket lay in its perfectly cut-out grave, covered with roses. My roses, she thought. The grass surrounding the gravestone was neatly clipped. She walked on it, searching, finally finding a small stone. She knelt to pick it up, went to the open grave and laid it among the roses. She was almost too tired for tears. Later she would come back alone. Later she would work out the grief. Later she would make sense of the life and death of the girl in the coffin. Now she was tired, beat. She turned back to the family, hugged Martina and the two husbands. Then she went home with them.

It was late in the afternoon when she awoke. The room was as familiar to her as the one she had grown up in thirty-five hundred miles away. It was the room they had given her on her first arrival and the room the little girl in the cemetery had relinquished for her on every visit. She had slept in it alone, with a husband, and again alone for the last several visits. A low murmuring sound came from downstairs. Visitors, she thought, sitting up.

There was a light rap on the door and Frau Biehl let herself into the room. "Did you sleep well?" she asked. She was wearing a black dress, and although her eyes were still puffy, she seemed to have acquired new energy since the morning.

"Thank you, very well." The eternal German exchange regarding sleep, like saying, "Hi, how are you?

Fine, thanks." A cultural courtesy.

"People have come to call."

"I'll wash and go downstairs."

Frau Biehl seemed in no hurry. She moved the only chair in the room and sat down. "When the end came, she was happy."

Lee felt her throat tighten, and nodded, saying nothing.

"She was my most beautiful child." The word, in German, did not necessarily mean "pretty," although it meant that, too. In this context, Lee understood it in its wider sense: the most wonderful child, the best child, the ultimate child, the child we were happiest to have.

"She was, yes."

"We were all together at the end." Frau Biehl glanced out the window into the gray afternoon sky. "Can you stay for a while?"

"Yes. I have a lot of vacation coming."

"Then you'll stay on after they leave." Meaning the daughters.

"I'll stay."

"Good." Frau Biehl stood. "There's coffee and cake downstairs."

"I'll be right down."

Death brings back the past. Every image, every scent, evoked an earlier echo of itself. The smell of the coffee and the sight of the delicate old coffee pot were enough to block out the crowd of murmuring friends and bring her back to those golden afternoons of coffee and cake after a day of classes at the university.

Often it was only the two of them, the mother and the American student, sitting together in the living room like ladies of another era, sipping, spreading whipped cream on freshly baked tortes, talking about war and peace and grammar and family life. Sometimes Marie-Luise or Martina would join them if their own classes had ended early. Only on weekends would the doctor be there, and then the conversation would be different, more political, encompassing religion and taxes.

"Are you the American?"

She turned, surprised to be addressed. The man was about her age or a little younger, good-looking, holding a cup of coffee in his hand.

"Yes."

"I'm Robert Becker," he added. "Marlies's old sweetheart." He said it with a wry twinkle.

"Robert." It was amazing. She could see the young Robert Becker in the face of this man.

"It's good to see you, Lee. It's been many years."

"Twenty."

"Yes, twenty. Tina was born after you left, wasn't she?"

"The following year."

"She was a great gift to this family."

Unexpectedly, her voice failed her. She swallowed hard. "She was a gift to everyone who knew her. It was good of you to come here this afternoon."

"I remember her as a baby." He set his cup and saucer on a nearby piece of furniture. "Are you married?"

"I was."

"Ah." He smiled with understanding although he could not possibly have understood. He had been a

11

handsome, charming boy who had adored Marlies for one whole year in high school and then become engaged to someone else not long after he went away to college. "Will you be here long?"

"A week or so."

"I hope you'll visit my wife and me. We have a house in town. Nothing special, but we'd like you to see it."

"Thank you, Robert. I'll try. I really will."

"Marie-Luise is still so beautiful, isn't she?"

Lee followed his eyes to where Marlies stood talking to a man and woman Lee had never seen. "Very beautiful," she said. "So are you, you know. Just the way you were."

She opened the French doors and went out to the patio. It was still a gray April day but the rain had stopped. The house was built high above the street, a hundred concrete steps to the plateau on which it sat. From this patio there was a view of the lower part of the town, the river that ran on the other side of the street, red slate roofs on the older houses, spires, hills farther away. It was a town of age and history. The great church down below in the center of town had been Catholic before the Reformation swept through and claimed it as its own. The original niches that had once held statues of saints were empty. The town had been reformed: it was Protestant, but the countryside had scarcely been touched and remained largely Catholic. The doctor had always been able to identify the religion of the women who wore their native costume into town in those days by how their hair was fixed and by the colors in their skirts. Not many of them dressed that way anymore. The young girls wanted to wear the latest fashions, use makeup, look like city girls. When they married, they wore white instead of the colorful traditional wedding costume of their mothers and grandmothers. *The old order changeth* . . .

"Aren't you cold?"

"Marty. Yes, I am a little cold. I was just thinking of how it used to be before they built all those little houses on the hill on the other side of town. It was so much prettier without them."

"That's what Daddy used to say."

"Did he know Tina was sick when he died?"

"I think he suspected it. We found out not long after. She died very peacefully, you know. Marlies and I got here just in time."

"Yes."

"She wasn't even as old as you when you came to us the first time."

"I know. A whole life in nineteen years."

They stood looking out over the scene. Sometimes on bright days in the summer, gliders used to pass overhead, their huge shadows darting across the grass, the flowers, the house itself. Today there were no shadows and no gliders.

"Come inside, Lee. It's much too cold out here."

It was true. She was chilled to the bone. She turned and went into the warmth and comfort of the living room.

The husbands departed the next morning after breakfast, one in a large Mercedes, the other in a

13

small German Ford. Their wives and sons remained behind, and scarcely had the car doors slammed at the bottom of the steps, than the atmosphere in the house changed. The two couples had gone down the stairs together, accompanied by their sons, but the sisters returned separately.

"Let's have another cup of coffee," Martina said when she came back to the dining room. "I made a big potful."

"Fine."

"You know we only have coffee for breakfast when you're here."

"I know and I've told your mother a hundred times it's not necessary. Tea is fine."

"It pleases her to do something special for you."

"It pleases me just to be here."

The front door opened and closed.

"Come and join us for a cup of coffee," Lee called to the unseen sister.

"I have some things to do, thanks," Marie-Luise called from the hallway. "See you later."

Lee looked at Martina.

She shrugged and smiled. "Perhaps I'm in the way this morning."

"No one's in the way in this house."

Martina's face turned inscrutable. She replaced the tea cozy on the pot and sipped her coffee. "Lee, I'm worried about Mummy. She's spent the last two years hovering over Tina and now there's nothing. How long do you think she can live in this house by herself?"

It was a big house, even for a whole family: a large master bedroom, a smaller one beside it, which the doctor had used when he was called out at night once in a while to attend an emergency, and four other bedrooms, including the maid's room, which hadn't been slept in by anyone except a grandchild for years. The sleep-in maids of yesteryear were long gone. Downstairs there were a kitchen, a living room, a dining room, and a cozy study. One woman in all of those rooms, one woman who had lost her husband, lost her youngest daughter.

"I don't know," Lee said. "It was a wonderful house when it was full."

"But it will never be full again. I would love to have her come to us, but our house is too small, much too small. And if she goes to Marlies . . . They don't get along that well, you know."

"I can't bear to think of this house being sold."

"Nor can I. But what will happen to Mummy if she stays here?"

"I don't know, Marty."

Marty's face broke into a beautiful smile. "You named me that, didn't you?"

"Yes, when I first came over. You were only twelve."

"And I loved it. It was so American, and everything about America seemed so wonderful. Everyone calls me that now. Except Mummy. You really had a big influence on our family."

It was hard to hold the tears back. She nodded but said nothing.

"Talk to Mummy, Lee. Ask her what she wants to do, where she wants to go. I know it's soon but she tells you things she doesn't tell us."

"I'll try."

"That's all I can ask."

15

Lee smiled. "Your coffee is super, you know that?"

"It's the filter paper. You should take some back with you, get yourself a new husband."

"Maybe I will."

So many things to remember. She took a walk after breakfast, slipping out by herself, sensing the tension in the house and not wanting to be part of it. She walked toward the center of town, passed through it, and started up the steep street that would take her, eventually, to the marketplace with the old fountain at its center. She passed the potter where she had bought small handmade pieces that even now stood on shelves in her New York apartment. The optician was still there but the leather goods store where she had bought a zipper case to hold her lecture notes was gone. New and old now alternated starkly. The whole rhythm of the street was wrong. It was neither ancient nor modern, but a careless mixture of both.

She felt the tug of unused muscles in her calves and stopped to catch her breath. There was a time when this had been a daily walk, a daily pleasure. Somewhere here on the left had been the old Mensa where they had eaten cheap, awful food for lunch and just beyond it the café where they paid more than the price of lunch for a cup of coffee and a piece of rich cake. She had never taken cream with her coffee, so they had given her a tiny cream pitcher full of coffee to balance the price. The Mensa was long gone, replaced with some modern monstrosity elsewhere in town, but the café was still there. She paused at the entrance but went on.

The bookstore. In the window a set of old books, perhaps a first edition. As a student she had not been able to afford such luxuries although she had looked, touched, reckoned her finances over and over to see if it might be a possibility. She could buy it now, even if it were expensive, but what would she buy?

She turned away from the window. She didn't want books or coffee or pottery. She wanted to go up, as high as she could, to the grounds of the castle. Walking briskly now she passed through the empty marketplace and found a little cobblestone street that slanted upward. Zigging and zagging she made her way through streets too narrow to accommodate cars and came, finally, breathlessly, to the last steps to the castle. Now the whole town lay below her, hundreds of red roofs, the river in the distance. She found a place to sit and drew her coat around her. It wasn't so much cold as clammy, and the sky was a deadly, unremitting gray. But the coat was warm and she folded her body into itself for comfort. Down below, if she kept the angle of her vision narrow, she could see only the old, the memorable, the beloved. From this vantage point, it might be twenty years ago or more.

Only it wasn't. Tina Biehl was dead. Lee Linden was back in Germany for her funeral. She let the tears come. They were long overdue.

Chapter Two

The American girl was a little too tall, a little too thin, and a little bit carried away by the thought of it all. A year abroad, a chance to study and travel, to have a good time, to perfect—at least improve—her German. Her grandparents had been horrified at the thought that a Jewish girl would select Germany when there were all those nice countries she could have gone to. When the fat letter came with the news that she had made it, that it would really happen, her grandfather had refused an invitation to dinner at the Steins'. Her grandmother had cried, but shortly before Lee's departure, she had given her a twenty-dollar bill which was to be spent in "some other country." Lee had promised she would spend it in France or England or maybe Denmark, which had been especially good to the Jews during the war.

Her parents had been one generation more enlightened. They, too, would have preferred France, but Lee had never studied French except to speak a few words, and the competition for England was fierce;

everyone had the language. The war was two decades gone and Germany was Israel's ally. It was time to accept that the world had changed.

For Lee Stein the decision had been much simpler. In high school they had begun offering German during her first year. She thought it would be so much nicer to learn a language that wasn't French. It had set her apart in an agreeable way. She quickly discovered she had an aptitude. Eventually, she took all the medals. In college it was easier to go on than to switch.

Standing at a window outside the expensive compartments as the train traveled the last miles to her destination, she felt the thrill of anticipation, the wonder that this was happening to her and not to someone else. The town was a painting out of a fairy tale. It was built on a hill with the castle on its peak, visible as the town first came into view. Church spires could be seen in the lower town, and houses set almost everywhere in between. A large public pool moved by fairly close, and the train slowed. The river flowed between the train and the city, a row of old houses lining its bank along one stretch like a picture of Venice.

She could feel the train braking now and she was suddenly a little scared. Someone would meet her and the small group of American students she was traveling with, but she didn't know who. She would be going to a house with two daughters, both younger than she. She had a letter from the older one, a high school girl kind of letter. At the last moment before the train stopped, her grandfather's fears rippled through her and became her own.

But there was no time for that. The platform was

gliding by outside the window, and the train was slowly coming to a stop. She went back to her seat and pulled her suitcase down from the rack, helping the others as they helped her, and got in line to get off.

The schoolteacher who had organized their lodging seemed to sense who they were as they stepped onto the platform.

"Miss Stein?" he asked in German-Oxford-accented English. "The Biehls are waiting for you. Come this way."

And there they were, three people whose faces glowed as she approached, standing as though for a formal portrait, Marlies with the very red cheeks that young girls so often had in this country, the doctor and his wife the picture of reserved, upstanding citizens with happy, welcoming eyes.

"I'm Lee Stein," she said in German, her eyes moving from one to the other and they greeted her with words and handshakes. She knew in a moment that her grandfather had been wrong. These were good people.

She fit into their lives as though they had been chosen for each other. They gave her the third bedroom, the one usually reserved for guests. Marie-Luise had the first, the one in the corner next to the maid's room, and Marty the second. The girls were six years apart, Frau Biehl told her one afternoon as they sat sipping coffee and eating cinnamon cake, but there was meant to be another child, halfway between them. Frau Biehl had given birth prematurely three years after Marlies's birth, and the child had not survived.

20

"It was the most difficult time of my life," Frau Biehl said, and her eyes misted. "When we built the house, we still thought there might be another child, but now—" She moved her hands as though to show that such thoughts had flown away with time. "So instead we have a guest from America."

In a way it was easier than living with her own parents. There was no sibling rivalry; she helped the daughters with their English assignments without being asked, and they were grateful for it. There was no parent-child friction. When she stayed out late, she asked Frau Biehl's permission (which she knew would always be forthcoming), so that Marlies would not follow too independent a model. Marlies would be in a university in two years and that would be time enough for her to assert herself. On the maid's day off, she joined Marlies in the kitchen to wash dishes and clean up, and they giggled and confided in each other like old friends. That was the year that Marlies loved Robert Becker.

Dr. Biehl was a gentle man who practiced surgery. He had a rigorous schedule of operating a few days a week and seeing patients in his office on other days. Once or twice a month the phone would ring in his bedroom in the middle of the night with news of an accident on the road and he would leave the house silently, sometimes turning up tired and unshaven at breakfast, sometimes returning before morning to catch up on his sleep. Frau Biehl would tell Lee at breakfast of the horrors of the accident. As if she were mother to all the victims, she shared their pain.

As the Steins were an unobservant Jewish family, the Biehls were an unobservant Catholic one. They paid their taxes to the Catholic Church but did not attend Mass. Dr. Biehl would complain about church taxes the way Lee's father complained about taxes in general.

They knew that she was Jewish from the start. She had written as much to Marie-Luise at her grandfather's urging so that they could reject her before she arrived and they tried to murder her. Marlies's answering letter had not mentioned anyone's religion, and Grandpa had said, with irritation, "All right, all right. Go already. What do I care?" She had written him as soon as she arrived, describing all four members of the family, but he had not yet answered. Perhaps he could not address a letter to a country called Germany.

When the subject arose, as it did in the first weeks of her stay, the Biehls spoke without hesitation about Germany and the Jews. They had known Jews—everyone had known Jews; they had been everywhere in the twenties and thirties—but they knew almost none today. There had been Jews in town before the war but few had returned afterward. They talked; she pressed questions on them; they answered.

There were nights when she went upstairs wondering what she would do if the police came and took away the man next door. Would she telephone and ask about it? What if they asked for her name, address, and telephone number? Would she have the guts to walk into the police station and demand to know what had happened to the missing man? She knew relatively little about the war, none of it from her own memory. Almost nothing had been taught in school; it had sort of been mentioned. Because she was Jewish, the Biehls seemed to think she was an expert on what had happened during the war years. Her only source of information was the World Almanac, which she dug out of her trunk and translated from liberally when they asked questions.

November first was All Saints' Day, and classes at the university began the following morning. She signed up for several classes that sounded intriguing: Superstition, Fairy Tales, the European Farmhouse. She had brought a tape recorder with her and she was anxious to find people with original, uncollected tales to tell. The Biehls could not help her. She would have to work through professors or, if they could not make connections, she would drive into the countryside and knock on doors. Her parents had ordered a Volkswagen for delivery on November fifteenth and as soon as that arrived, she could begin.

On the Sunday evening after the university had opened for the fall semester, she sat in Marlies's room as Marlies prepared for the next day's English class. She had to read a short story and answer questions about it. She read well but slowly, stopping to look up words that were unfamiliar.

Suddenly, she put the book down and spoke in German. "Lee, there's a boy in my English class."

Lee smiled. "And?"

"He's wonderful. He's the most beautiful-looking person I've ever seen in my life."

"You're rather beautiful yourself, you know."

Marlies blushed. "I think he likes me."

"That's wonderful."

"I'll point him out to you on Wednesday night."

"Wednesday night?"

"Didn't Mummy tell you?"

"Tell me what?"

"The theater season is starting. We always go to the premiere. You'll come with us, as our guest, of course. Mummy will mention it tomorrow."

"What sort of plays do they do?"

"Everything you can think of. Shakespeare, Molière, everything."

"In German?"

"Oh, yes, everything in German. Marty won't come. She's still too young. But Robert will be there. He told me on Friday."

"Well, don't point with your finger. Your mother said it's bad manners. What shall I wear?"

"Mummy will probably wear silk, but you and I just have to look like ladies."

"I wonder if I'll be able to do that," Lee teased.

Marlies laughed. "Of course you can. Wear the white silk blouse and the tight black skirt. You'll look wonderful."

"You know all my clothes."

"I couldn't possibly know all your clothes, you have so many of them. And wear those black shoes with the tiny heel. It doesn't matter that you're taller than Daddy."

"Whatever you say, Fräulein Biehl. And would you like to polish my fingernails for me?"

"Good heavens, no. Daddy will throw you out. He has *very* strong opinions about painted fingernails."

Frau Biehl told her about the play the next morning and she accepted the invitation gratefully. Her social life here was very different from the social life at school in the States. Here she lunched with her American friends and an occasional German whom one of them might bring along. In her classes, the German students were friendly but reserved. The person she was closest to outside the Biehl family was Sally Gordon, a student of sociology who had come with her husband and three-year-old daughter. Sam, the husband, stayed home with the child most of the time, working on his novel, while Sally went to classes and socialized with other students in a most carefree way. They were a conspicuous anomaly among the traditional families in town. Sally and Sam would not be at the theater. They were saving their money for travel during the generous German vacations.

On Wednesday, after a supper of bread, smoked eel, ham, cheese, and liverwurst, they dressed and went to the town theater in the doctor's car. Marty pouted at being left behind, but Frau Biehl shooed her upstairs to work on her homework as they left.

The performance was *Othello* with the lead played by a big German actor in blackface. Listening to the German and trying to match the phrases to what she knew of the English was a challenge for Lee. Most arduous was just trying to understand the lines as they were delivered.

The end of the first act came as a relief. Now, for a little while, she could listen to the more prosaic and easily understood German of the family.

They took a position in the large lobby, Frau Biehl nodding and smiling as people met her eyes. A middle-aged couple stopped to say hello, and Frau Biehl introduced Marlies and then said, "And this is our American, Miss Stein."

Lee shook hands with the couple, whose name she had not caught, smiled, and said, "Good evening." They moved away and the doctor returned with sweets.

Suddenly, Lee felt Marlies clutch her hand. "There he is," she said under her breath without turning her head.

"Where?"

"Near the pillar. With his parents. A tall man and a short woman?"

"Yes. I see."

"Was I right? Is he beautiful?"

"Very. Let's walk over and you can introduce me as your American."

"No."

"All right."

"Did you say something, Marlies?" Frau Biehl asked.

"No, Mummy." She was still holding Lee's hand tightly. "Mummy, Lee and I are going to talk to someone."

"Don't be too long. There's only a few minutes left."

"We'll see you inside." She tugged at Lee and they started walking. As they moved through the crowd, she composed herself, her cheeks receding to their ordinary redness, her body erect, emulating her mother's carriage. "Good evening, Robert," she said as they came upon the threesome.

There was no mistaking the look of true love in Robert's eyes. He introduced her to his parents and then Marlies introduced Lee. "This is Lee Stein who is visiting us this year from America."

Lee shook three sets of hands and answered questions about the university.

"We hope our Robert will study in America one day," Frau Becker said. "The well-rounded student should learn another language well and make connections abroad, don't you think so, Miss Stein?"

It would have been hard to say anything but yes. Dutifully, she said what was expected.

Frau Becker smiled with satisfaction. "You see, Robert," she began, but the lights blinked as she spoke. "Ah, the second act. How nice to meet you, Miss Stein."

The five of them turned toward the theater doors, Robert and Marlies moving off together, speaking and smiling for a moment until their directions separated them.

Marlies was still glowing when she joined Lee. "He's coming over tomorrow evening," she said. "To work on English. The three of us can work together, all right?"

"Sure it's all right. Am I a tutor or a matchmaker?"

"A tutor, of course. Lee, I think this is going to be the best year of my life."

"That makes two of us," Lee said.

It was during the second intermission that she saw Frau Dierich for the first time. They were standing near one of the large pillars when Frau Biehl leaned over and said, "The people to the left of the door. Frau Dierich is a Jew."

Lee looked quickly. As she saw the man, woman,

and teenage son, the woman moved her head, saw Frau Biehl, and smiled. Frau Biehl smiled and nodded as she had all evening.

"She was in a camp during the war. The son was born when she came back. He's a year older than Marie-Luise. You know him, don't you, Marlies?"

"He goes to our school. He wants to study law. He walked me home from a party once last year."

Lee looked at Frau Dierich with fascination, a Jewish woman who had been in a camp and had returned to the German city she had been taken from to continue her life, to give life to a son who would grow up here. "Was her husband taken away too?"

"I don't think so," Frau Biehl said. "I think he lost his job but he's doing very well now."

One could see that it was true. They were well-dressed without the dowdiness of many of the women, and Frau Dierich, although simply clothed, had a glitter here and there that was surely jewelry.

"I wonder why she came back," Lee said.

"Her husband was here. Her home was here."

Home and husband. A couple stopped where the Dierichs stood and chatted politely with them, then moved on.

"I wouldn't have come back," Lee said.

"You're young and you don't have a husband. Where should she have gone? To another country? Learn a new language? She has a good husband who waited for her. She's probably alive today because of him. The other people, where they were both Jews, they didn't come back."

"But she must have been arrested by a policeman she knew from town or a soldier she used to see walking to school. Imagine coming back and seeing him again."

"Soldiers and policemen are the same everywhere. In uniform they have power. Without the uniform they are ordinary people."

The lights began to blink and the Biehls started for the theater. Lee kept her eyes on Frau Dierich. She was a small woman, older than Frau Biehl. Lee searched her face for signs of the horror that she must have experienced, but the face looked no different from the other female faces in the crowd except that perhaps it was finer. It was not lined, not gaunt, not scarred. The eyes were soft. Only around the mouth there was something she could not identify. The mouth looked older than the rest of the face.

Before they reached the door, the three Dierichs had gone inside. When Lee and Marlies passed through the door, they were gone.

Robert Becker came to visit the next evening, and for half an hour of that time, Lee joined them in Marie-Luise's bedroom. They worked on English and laughed and talked. Robert insisted on addressing Lee with the formal "Sie" instead of the informal "Du." When he had gone, she told Marlies that that was silly. They were all the same generation and should address each other as such. Marlies said she would pass along the message.

The professors treated her with courtesy but did not take her very seriously. They suggested that she study

29

at least for a semester, preferably more, before going out into the field looking for original folktales.

"I'll only be here for a year," she said to one of them. "I'd really like to get started."

"I have students studying much longer than you, and they have found it hard to make such contacts. Patience is very important in this discipline."

But she had neither patience nor time. Once the car was delivered, she had the means to travel, but she realized she could not drive aimlessly, stopping farmers in the field. She needed an entrance and the academic community had circled its wagons.

In the end it was Sally Gordon who made it all happen. They were having coffee at the café after a particularly tasteless soupy mixture for lunch at the Mensa when Lee blurted out her problem.

"It's like a conspiracy of silence," she said glumly. "And my so-called colleagues, the other students, are worse than the professors. The professors think I should study for half my life before I go into the field; the students just don't want to give me any tips on finding informants. All they're willing to say is that someone they know pointed them in the right direction."

"We'll ask Fräulein Doktor Wirter. She'll help," Sally said.

"Why will she help?"

"Because I'll twist her arm. She's a sociologist, not a folklorist. It costs her nothing to help. She's told me about a village near here that an American couple wrote a book about a few years go. She was their contact. I'll bring her around tomorrow for coffee."

"Do I have to call her Fräulein Doktor?"

30

"Of course you do. You haven't been friends for twenty-five years yet, have you?"

"Not likely," Lee said with a smile. "How's Sam doing on his novel?"

"Wonderfully. And he's turned out to be the world's best mother. For him Wendy takes a long nap in the afternoon, for me never. For him Wendy eats whatever he puts in front of her. For Sam, Wendy plays with other children and lets him write in peace. We should have done this from the start. I wonder how his mother's milk is." She looked thoughtful.

Lee burst into laughter. "I have seen the future and it's Sally Gordon," she said.

"You better believe it," Sally told her.

Fräulein Doktor Wirter was a thin, plain, spinster woman probably in her early thirties. She wore thick glasses and although she looked very intense, she smiled frequently and encouragingly. She made some phone calls, which led to an appointment, and together they traveled to a small village about eighteen kilometers from town on a gray morning in late November.

They went first to the church, which was the tallest building in the village, and spoke to the priest for about half an hour. He remembered Fräulein Doktor Wirter very well from her work with the Americans. He knew an old man, yes, who might he willing to talk to Lee, but the old man didn't come to church much and might not take it well if the priest called. Perhaps she should first go to Frau Möck who lived at number nineteen; she would be home today unless it was her turn at the bread oven.

Fräulein Doktor Wirter thanked him profusely, and Lee added the most grammatically gracious sentence she could manage. Then they went off to see Frau Möck.

The whole adventure had begun in the kitchen of that ancient house, sitting at the wooden table with those pink-cheeked women in their native costume, the last generation that would wear it. In that kitchen a remarkable friendship developed and grew in the warmth of the fire in the woodstove.

Chapter Three

It was really too cold to sit so long without moving. Lee stood and pulled a silk scarf from her coat pocket, tied it around her head and then pulled the ends across her neck to knot at the back. Then she put gloves on and started to walk. The castle grounds were still bleak with leftover winter.

What a winter that had been twenty years ago. Marie-Luise and Robert had fallen in love, in a rather sweet, childlike way at first, then more and more seriously. And every week Lee would drive out to the little village, stopping now and then to allow geese or a small herd of sheep to cross the road, and sit in the old kitchen sipping real coffee with real cream and eating too much buttercream cake which Frau Möck had baked for her that morning. Frau Möck delivered the old man with the wonderful stories, but by springtime she had given Lee much more.

"Much more," Lee said aloud to no one but herself. So much in one year, so much unexpected.

It had been so long since she had sat and thought

about that year, thought about it in a chronological way: first this happened, then that happened. And of course in the spring, just at the change of seasons, she had met Rich and everything in her life had been different after that. What a long time it had been since she had thought of him.

It was almost hard to see him in this weather. Rich had been springtime. Rich had been summer. Closing her eyes against the wind, she could see him outlined against the sky.

He was a man who loved a ruin the way some men love a fine cigar or a special blend of whiskey. He inhaled them; he imbibed them. He felt enriched by them. There was one bona fide ruin at the edge of town and they went there that first, wonderful weekend, the time he stayed over at the Gordons'. It was the ruin of a castle built by a noblewoman for her daughter some half a dozen centuries earlier. The daughter had died before the castle was completed and had never lived in it. All that was left was a shell full of gaping holes so that there was more light than darkness inside. There always seemed to be a breeze there. Whenever she went, which had been often during that year, her skirt blew and her hair was tousled.

Rich had stood at one of the high interior points, at the edge of a huge, windowlike hole, and looked out at the countryside. It was almost too easy to love a man like that, the way he stood, lost in that special rapture, the way the sun picked up the crystal of his watch and turned it into a flash of light, the way his arms, bare from the summer sleeve down, looked so strong and could be so gentle. He turned and saw her and smiled. Rich in the early, wonderful days.

The wind blew and stung her cheeks. It was time to go home.

"Look at you, you look like a piece of ice," Frau Biehl said as Lee stepped inside the house, breathless from her climb up the stairs.

"I feel like one."

"I would have given you a sweater. You never dress warmly enough. It's still cold here."

"Where did you go?" Marty asked, taking Lee's coat and hanging it up.

"To the castle."

"My goodness," Frau Biehl said. "You must be frozen stiff. We'll have soup for dinner. Marie-Luise has cooked for us today."

It was a warm, nourishing meal. The soup was delicious. After it came a rump steak with potatoes and a green salad served on small glass plates.

Frau Biehl went upstairs for her daily nap when dinner was over.

"Let me wash up," Lee said when she was gone.

"Nonsense," Marty said, rising and clearing the table. "Marlies cooked and I'll take care of the rest. With the dishwasher, it's really nothing anyway. Go upstairs and lie down. You look as though you could use a rest. We'll have coffee when Mummy wakes up. Marlies baked you a cinnamon cake this morning."

"You're too good to me."

"You look as though you could use a few calories," Marlies said. Then she motioned with her finger for Lee to follow.

They went upstairs to her old room at the corner of

the house. The second bed had already been removed since the husbands' departures. From the room next door came little giggling sounds; Marlies's sons were there, too old for a nap but not allowed to run around the house at this time and make noise.

"There are problems between Mummy and me," Marlies said. She had propped herself on pillows so that Lee could sit on the desk chair.

"I'm sorry to hear it."

"Kurt has other interests."

It came as a surprise. "I find that hard to believe."

"I found it even harder."

"I'm so sorry."

"Mummy says I'm to blame."

"Your mother has old-fashioned values. You mustn't think . . ."

"It hurts me so much to have her blame me. I've been a good wife."

"I know you have."

Marlies wiped her eyes. "Nothing's been the same around here since Daddy died. I only visited because of Tina. Tina was the first baby I ever held, the first I ever took care of. I was nearly twenty when Mummy brought her home. I was old enough to be her mother."

"She was lucky to have you."

"These have been terrible years."

"I know."

"Lee." Marlies moved to make herself comfortable. "You were divorced. What happened in your marriage?"

There are questions one doesn't want to answer because they nibble at the core of buried truths. "I kept too much of myself to myself," she said.

"That isn't like you. You and I were the same. We had no secrets. When I met Kurt, he knew everything there was to know about me and he loved me."

"I was older when I married and so much had happened, so much that I couldn't talk about." Even now, she thought. Even now I can't talk about it.

Marlies looked at her silently. Next door the giggling had stopped. Perhaps the younger brother had fallen asleep. "Go to sleep, Lee," she said finally. "You look all worn out."

On the first day that Lee had gone alone to Frau Möck's house, Frau Möck and the two sisters-in-law — whose names and relationships never became clear to Lee — sat and talked in the kitchen with the tape recorder running. The three German women had listened back in awe to their voices, laughing, covering their mouths, amazed at the sound. Each was assured by the others that the representation of her voice was accurate. None believed it of her own.

Then, having let them enjoy the tape recorder and having in turn enjoyed their coffee and cake, she asked each to tell a fairy tale. The stories were familiar — Hansel and Gretel, Little Red Riding Hood. They delivered them not in standard German but in the dialect of the village. Frau Möck was a real artist. Her voice was strong and clear, slightly high-pitched. She took the parts of the witch and the children like an actress reading for a part. The recording was beautiful.

When they were done and Lee was ready to go she

said, "I've heard that there's an old man around here who tells wonderful ghost stories."

The women's faces lit up. "Peter," one said. "Old Peter," from another.

Yes, Frau Möck said, she could have him here next Wednesday. She would speak to him herself tomorrow morning.

"You got him in one shot?" Sally Gordon said, with obvious admiration.

"Just by asking. And they're all looking forward to it. He must be some character."

"You may end up with a bookful of stories from this one guy."

"But then I need to find out whether those stories are specific to this area or whether there are altered versions in other places."

"You'll need five years. Three anyway. Are you prepared?"

"I'll worry about it later. How's Sam's novel coming?"

"Blossoming. Sometimes he works so hard he forgets to cook dinner."

Old Peter was indeed a character. He looked like a combination of an elf and a farmer. He told Lee two stories in a dialect so thick she could understand almost nothing. He laughed uproariously at the funny parts, along with the women, clapped his hands at a stroke of thunder and changed his voice for each character. Two little children, hearing his voice, crept into the kitchen to listen.

She carried the tape recorder to the next meeting of her course in superstition. At the end of the hour, she played Frau Möck telling Hansel and Gretel.

The professor listened intently. He was old and very sweet. He half-believed in the superstitions he lectured about because he had seen them work firsthand.

When Frau Möck's story was finished, he said, "It's not original. Did you hear her mention chocolate? That's modern. She was repeating a story she had read in a book or heard. I'm sorry, Fräulein Stein."

"Do you have time to listen to another?"

"Of course," he said kindly.

She turned on the tape recorder and Old Peter's highpitched voice took over the room. A cluster of students had gathered. Among them was one who had refused to help her a month ago. She watched the faces as they listened.

The professor was all smiles. "I would like to meet this Peter," he said from his chair. "That was an original story. A very good one."

"I'll try to arrange it," Lee said.

"Where are you from, Fräulein Stein?"

"America."

"America, yes. How does an American girl find an old man with original stories when I can't find them myself?"

"I had a little help."

"Even so," the professor said. "Even so."

It was too close to Christmas so she arranged the meeting for January. Marie-Luise was invited to the

39

Christmas dance by Robert, and Lee and another American joined the Gordons for a trip to Holland. They celebrated the new year in Amsterdam with an American family the Gordons knew from home. Sally and Sam seemed very happy to be away from Germany. Sally became mother again and Sam did the driving, just like an ordinary American family.

There are no ordinary families, Lee thought, sitting up in bed. She had slept for about twenty minutes, then lain under the covers thinking. There was nothing ordinary about the Biehls. They had been the most beautiful family she had ever known, warm and loving and considerate of each other, and now what had happened? She could not believe that Marlies's husband had "other interests." She could not believe that Frau Biehl would blame her daughter for her husband's behavior.

There was a knock on the door and she called, "Come in."

Frau Biehl came in, dressed and rested. "You look better now. Will you have coffee?"

"Of course."

"We have cinnamon cake for you. Afterward Marlies and Martina will go shopping for supper."

And we will be alone to talk, Lee thought. She washed in the sink in her bedroom and dressed quickly. The time had finally come when they would talk.

The daughters took the three sons with them. A

40

walk in the city would do them good after being cooped up in the house for several days.

Frau Biehl poured the last of the coffee. "I wanted you to be here," she said, setting the pot down. "But the end came very quickly."

"I understand."

"She loved you, Lee."

Lee nodded. On her first visit to Germany after Tina's birth, she had brought American overalls and little shirts with appliquéd flowers. Tina had been a round, bouncy baby, a happy child. She must have the photographs somewhere, a little girl in a shirt with a sunflower.

"You and I will always be friends, won't we?" Frau Biehl asked. "Even without Tina?"

"Of course we will."

"I am losing my other daughters."

"You won't lose them."

"I lost them a long time ago. They only came here for Tina."

"Marty is worried about you staying here alone."

"No one is worried about me. Tina worried. Tina was my best child." Her voice shook.

A little round baby in American overalls.

"Another piece of cake?" Frau Biehl said, asserting her will over her emotions.

"No, thank you."

"You're too thin. You won't get married if you stay so thin. A man has to have something to hold."

Lee smiled.

"That man—did you ever see him again? What was his name?"

"Rich. I never saw him again."

41

"You should have tried. He was the right man for you."

Tears spurted unexpectedly. She had thought she would cry when they talked about Tina but she was crying now and they were talking about Rich. "I don't break up people's marriages," she said.

"The marriage was already broken. He told me that."

"He told you he was married?"

"We talked once when he came to see you. You were upstairs dressing. He wanted me to know about him because in Germany I was like your mother. He wanted me to trust him. I liked that man. He was a good man for you."

A small discovery twenty years later. She wiped her face with a tissue. "I didn't know he told you," she said.

In the evening they spread their rye bread or black bread with butter and covered it with a slice of cheese or smoked ham. Tina used to sit on this side of the table, Lee thought, looking around. There, where Marty's little boy was sitting. Sometimes she would break the rules and put two slices of ham or cheese on one slice of bread. That wasn't allowed. Smoothing the butter over her bread, Lee remembered that she too had broken the rules. She had eaten ham or cheese without any bread.

"If you don't eat bread tonight, you'll be cold tomorrow," Frau Biehl's voice sounded from twenty years before. "Wait and see."

She had never been cold, not one day of the winter.

* * *

She looked out the French door that was the only window in the bedroom. There was a glow in the night sky and lights here and there. The night was remarkably clear. The mist would be back in the morning, the mist that made this house and the plateau on which it stood seem like a world cut off from the rest of humanity.

Rich. Always when she remembered that year there was Rich. She would push away the memory so that she could remember the Biehls and Frau Möck and Old Peter, and Robert Becker who wouldn't say "Du" to her until the proper ceremony had been enacted. Rich had told Frau Biehl about his marriage. She had always known he was honorable. Imagine her not telling that to Lee for twenty years. She even remembered which day it must have been, when she was upstairs letting Marlies help her into the dress that needed a dozen buttons fastened up the back. Rich had been the one experience in her life of blind, unthinking passion, and she had spent all the intervening years trying to make it happen again. Maybe you had to be in your early twenties for that to happen. Maybe you had to be fresh out of college. Maybe you had to be in another country . . .

She pulled the curtain across the French doors and got into bed. Tonight she could not push him away. Tonight he was here with her, close, touching. I remember everything, she thought, every moment we spent together, every kindness, every gentle touch. Which of the weekends was the best? She could see the two of them in all the wonderful places they had vis-

43

ited, cafés where they had drunk a glass of wine, rooms they had made love in. Like the pictures they had never taken, she saw snapshots of them, Lee and Rich together in a hundred happy places.

I have a great ruin for you this weekend. It's across the Rhine from Bonn. A little town called Königswinter Drachenfels.

And she had said it in English, *Dragon Rock*.

If there was a best, that was it, when we knew it was real, when we started talking about the future as though it meant something beyond next weekend or next month. I've been married and I've had a lover or two I thought was pretty terrific, but I've never felt about anyone the way I felt about Rich that weekend, when being near him was almost painful because I loved him so much.

She lay on Tina Biehl's pillow and saw him, her Rich. I had him for such a short time, she thought, but for that time he was mine. The only man that ever really was.

Chapter Four

Sometimes she would see Frau Dierich in the city. Once she was carrying a bag of groceries; once she was leaving the hairdresser's that Frau Biehl went to weekly and Lee monthly for a haircut. The three Dierichs were at the opening of every new play. Lee wondered at her own fascination. Was the son being brought up a Jew? Was Frau Dierich content to live here or did she stay because her husband had a business which he could not leave? Once, when she saw her in the street, Lee nearly crossed over to talk to her. But what would she say? Hello, I'm Lee Stein. I'm from America and I'm a Jew. The woman would think her odd at best. Maybe she would think much worse. Perhaps she didn't want it known that she was Jewish. Lee watched the small, pretty woman walk by and went on her way.

"Robert, it's ridiculous for us to say 'Sie' to each other. Can't we just drop it?"

Robert closed the book of English poetry. "We have to do it the right way," he said. "This is serious business, you know. Next time I come to see Marlies, we'll have a little ceremony."

Marlies was all smiles. Lee knew that when she wasn't there, they held hands, moving quickly away from each other when she entered the room. She could hear rustlings after she knocked on the door. "Must I dress specially for this ceremony?" she asked.

"Well, of course," Robert said. "Jeans will never do."

"All right, Robert. Next time you come."

The day that she took Professor Holder out to the village to meet Old Peter it rained. The professor's daughter, a single woman in her thirties, answered the door and immediately expressed fears for her father's safety.

"The roads will be terrible," she said with a worried look. "Do you know them well?"

"I go there frequently. I've been there in worse weather than this."

"My father is very old," she said.

"I'll be very careful, Fräulein Holder. I never drive fast."

"Germans do."

"I know, but I don't."

She seemed reassured. When her father came out of his room, she straightened his tie, helped him on with his coat, and kissed him. Then she stood at the window watching them leave.

The professor entertained her during the drive with bits of folklore about the area. Certain kinds of supernatural creatures were indigenous to certain geographical areas but not to others. This was a fairly safe place to live although appearances of spooks were not unknown. He asked her if the place she lived in in the United States was safe.

"I think so," she said, wondering if this were a joke.

"Do you have ghosts there?" he asked.

"No."

"Giants?"

"I've never seen any."

He nodded. "Very safe," he said. "Very safe territory. A good place to live, the United States."

He was impressed with Old Peter. Peter had seen one ghost when he was a boy and from then on, people had reported sightings to him. There was a wooded area between this village and the next that he would not walk through at night and generally skirted even in daylight. Terrible things had been known to happen there.

The three village women sat at the kitchen table listening with wide eyes and clenched fists. The tape recorder ran, picking up the occasional comment or gasp from the sidelines. Lee sat feeling a happiness, a contentment, she had not felt since her arrival. The women liked and accepted her. The professor was impressed with her accomplishment. She would go home with original, publishable material. Already Frau Möck had given her the name and address of a woman in another village, someone who might be able to continue her search. She drove the professor home to his smiling, relieved daughter, feeling satisfied and eager to continue. She had a new idea for her next trip to the village. She was a little nervous about it but she couldn't wait to try.

When Robert came to visit Marlies a week later, he carried something in a cotton net bag. It turned out to be a split of *Sekt*, the German sparkling wine.

"We'll drink *Brüderschaft*," he announced, unwrapping the bottle.

"I'll get some glasses," Marlies said, running off to the china cabinet in the dining room. She returned with two beautiful crystal goblets.

"This makes it even more serious," Robert said. "If we break a glass, I may never be allowed in this house again."

They carried everything upstairs and Robert uncorked the bottle. "I have a little speech," he said, pulling a folded sheet of paper from his corduroy pants pocket.

Lee and Marie-Luise burst into laughter.

"Please," he said, trying to keep a straight face. He poured the wine into the glasses, lifted one, and read his speech. It sounded like something an ambassador would say to a foreign counterpart. It was full of sentiments of good will and friendship and mutual understanding. He nodded to Lee as he finished.

She picked up the second glass and said, "I am

deeply touched. I look forward to being your friend, Robert." Being careful to use the polite form for the last time.

They linked right arms and emptied their glasses. Little Marty had poked her head inside the room to watch and she cheered them on.

When the *Sekt* had been drunk, they both laughed.

"*Du,* Robert," Lee said.

"*Du,* Lee."

Marty was watching with childlike envy. "I hope I get to do that some day," she said.

"You will," Lee promised. "Many times."

Robert Becker, who had come to the Biehls' after Tina's funeral. *Du,* Robert, she thought. You have really been a friend.

The funeral had been on Wednesday and the husbands had left on Thursday. The daughters were staying through the weekend although each of them said from time to time that she was needed at home. Lee tried to help with household tasks, but they would not have it. Between them, they had taken charge, and Frau Biehl, a characteristically energetic and involved woman, spent much time in her room or in the study with the door closed.

On Friday after breakfast the sun began to shine through the clouds, and Lee left the sisters with the dishes. She put her coat on and walked toward town. The sisters were avoiding each other and while each proclaimed her concern for their mother, Frau Biehl had said she had lost them both. The family, the perfect, wonderful family of twenty years ago, had disintegrated into three separate strands like a thick cord that had unraveled into three insubstantial strings.

She walked through the lower city, in and out of old streets with narrow old houses. It was a long walk to the cemetery and she had to stop someone once to ask directions. When she got there, she followed the roadway the taxi had taken two days earlier, through the old section with its fading stones to the new, and across the grass to the stone with Dr. Biehl's name on it and a fresh grave in front.

The sight of the grave stung her. "My lovely Tina," she said in a low voice. "How could you have lived only nineteen years?" It was only a moment ago that she had been crawling on the Biehls' floor in her American sunflower outfit.

She had been a good student from everything Lee had heard. She would have had her choice of universities. At the time that illness had struck, Lee had written offering to watch over Tina if she came to an American university to study. But she wound up never going to any. Frau Biehl had been afraid to let her go away from home even while Marie-Luise and Marty had championed their sister's right to a semester of happiness.

They had all been right and all been wrong. Tina would have loved that semester, but the disease had reasserted itself at a time that would have cut the semester cruelly short. Perhaps if not under the eagle eye of her mother, she would not have sought help quickly enough and shortened her life even further.

I should have brought flowers, Lee thought, although there were still fresh flowers from the burial, many fresh flowers.

"I thought you might be here."

Startled, Lee turned to see Frau Biehl. "You should have called a taxi. It's a long walk from the house."

"You know me. I walk a lot. I've always enjoyed walking. It's a beautiful spot, isn't it?"

"Very beautiful."

"The sun falls on it almost all day long. We'll have her name put on one side of the cross. Mine will go on the other."

"You know how much I share your grief."

"I know." She walked closer to the grave and looked at the flowers, kneeling to see them more closely. "My husband's colleagues at the hospital all sent flowers. I've been writing notes to thank them and sending the death notices. He worked too hard, my husband. He took everyone's problems more seriously than his own. Two days before his heart attack he was out at three in the morning when a young man's car hit a tree. The young man stank of beer, but it didn't matter to my husband. He operated because there was a patient who needed him. The young man lived. Two days later my husband was dead. Perhaps . . ." She stood erect and stepped back from the grave.

" 'Perhaps' is the biggest word in any language."

"That's true. Everything would be different if my husband were alive. Has Marie-Luise told you about

51

Kurt?"

"A little. I feel very bad about it. She said you and she were in disagreement about it."

Frau Biehl shook her head and smiled. "We have no disagreements about her husband. Our disagreements are about money."

Lee was stunned. "No," she said.

"Yes," Frau Biehl said firmly. "She doesn't like the way I manage my husband's money. Marlies is a rich woman with an unhappy life. She wants to be richer and thinks it would make her happier. Her sister has very little money and is the happiest person in the world, but she wishes she had more money. There's envy between them."

"I don't believe it."

"But it's true. If you knew—"

"Please. I don't want to know."

Frau Biehl walked to a wreath of flowers and started pulling out the fading ones. "Do you remember what a happy family this was?"

"I remember well. I was part of it."

"Since this child died, this family is gone. It doesn't exist. I am alone."

"You're not alone, Frau Biehl."

Frau Biehl looked at her with eyes that were full. "Thank you, my friend," she said.

The village that Lee traveled to that year was out of another time. Houses were numbered and the streets had no names. They were narrow and cobbled; children ran down the center as if they owned

52

them—which they did. Cars were infrequent. Trucks were unheard of. In the morning the men left for work in the city and in the evening they returned. Otherwise, there was little commerce. When Lee arrived, by some amazing coincidence almost every housewife in sight of Frau Möck's house was sweeping her front walk as though they did it daily at exactly that hour.

Once she came on a Tuesday instead of a Wednesday and caught some of them unawares. She wondered if they listened for the sound of the little red Volkswagen as it rounded the bend and came into the village.

On that Tuesday there was a surprise for her in the house, too. Spread out on the floor under a window was a row of freshly baked loaves of bread. Tuesday was Frau Möck's baking day at the village oven. In the morning she brought the formed loaves of dough and later she collected the finished breads. A different townswoman was on duty each day to see that the breads did not burn and to remove them when they were finished.

Lee knew without being told that it was the end of an era. When Frau Möck and her sisters-in-law were gone, there would be no one to wear the native costume. The houses would all have flush toilets and electric stoves. The coal stoves Frau Möck had shown her in the upstairs bedrooms would be no more than laughable antiques or rusty trash. And the memories would be gone, too, the memories she was now determined to collect and preserve forever.

The village was almost entirely Catholic and Frau

Möck had opened her home and kitchen to Lee because Lee had been sent by the priest. The priest was mentioned frequently around the kitchen table as an authority, not only on matters of religion.

"Our priest," Frau Möck had said on the first afternoon that Lee had visited, "is a very smart man. Are you Catholic?"

"No," Lee had said and before she could add anything, Frau Möck had continued, "Ah, you're Protestant."

It was a comment that Lee had come to anticipate. In Germany there were only two choices of religion. If you didn't own up to one, you were assumed to be the other. Something of her grandfather's fears had kept her from correcting the false conclusions. The Biehls seemed to care not at all that she was Jewish, but what of other people? How would this farmer's wife in a remote little Catholic village feel about sharing her kitchen with a Jew?

When she visited a week after taking Professor Holder to the Möck house, she asked Frau Möck if she remembered the war. There were murmurs from the sisters-in-law and a strong *yes* from Frau Möck. Lee turned on the tape recorder and let her speak. Out came tales of shortages, of working in the fields without their men, of the appearance, at the very end of the war, of American soldiers in tanks, of the first time they saw a Negro soldier and the priest's warnings about them.

Lee asked few questions. Frau Möck's memory was delicious and Lee savored it. When she listened back over the next few days, transcribing the tape on her typewriter, she felt excitement. Buried in one of the recollections was a sentence about the Jew, Mandelbaum, who had been taken away. Old Peter and the ghost stories could wait; Frau Möck was going to tell her even better tales. These would be real.

The following week she arrived early.

"Did you like my fairy tales last week?" Frau Möck asked, making a joke.

"Better even than Hansel and Gretel. Would you mind if I asked you some more?"

Frau Möck was all smiles. In the center of the table was a beautiful chocolate cake and the cups and saucers were already stacked at one end.

Lee flicked on the tape recorder. "You said last week that Herr Mandelbaum was taken away. Were there other Jews in the village?"

"Oh yes," Frau Möck said with her usual enthusiasm. "I remember Frau Weinberger. She was an old woman. She lived in number thirty-one or thirty-three. Her son had left the country."

"Where did he go?"

"Canada," one of the sisters-in-law said. "Heinzel Weinberger was his name. He went to Canada. Wrote to his mother from there. I remember. She showed me the stamp."

"Were there others?" Lee asked softly.

"There was Rubenstein," Frau Möck said. "He used to come to the door with buttons and thread and dress material. There was Handelmann."

"The tailor," the second sister-in-law chimed in.

"What was his name? Frenkel!" she said with delight. "Remember Frenkel? Remember the time his chicken got stolen?"

"What happened to them?" Lee asked.

"They didn't come back," Frau Möck said. "Not one. They all didn't come back." She sat back in her chair, looking sad and thoughtful. "One came back. Leo. But he was from another town."

"Was there a synagogue?" Lee asked, her voice still very low, as though by keeping it low she could keep the flow of memories from being interrupted.

"Of course there was a synagogue. Across the road." Frau Möck pointed toward the living room which was at the front the house. "Behind the blacksmith shop. I remember the night the men came and destroyed it."

She felt a chill now, down her back and along her arms. Even her cheeks prickled. "Do you remember when that was?" she asked.

"I can never forget it. I was upstairs in my bedroom giving birth to my first son. November ninth. The year was nineteen thirty-eight."

"What happened that night?" Almost a whisper.

"There was noise, so much noise. Shouting. Oma," she pointed to the little round old woman who was always there, whose constant smile revealed few teeth, a woman whose dark skirt fell nearly to her ankle, whose hair was streaked with gray but still largely black in spite of her obvious years, "Oma went across the road to see what was going on. There were men with masks in the synagogue. 'What are you doing here?' she asked them, and one of them hit her. Like this." Frau Möck demonstrated with her right arm, a fierce blow. "Oma came home, but we heard the noise for a long time, windows breaking, loud voices. Later my son was born. They were from another village, those men. They weren't from here."

"They hit me."

Lee turned. In the little shed that adjoined the kitchen, a room with a dirt floor and no interior walls, the old woman sat and peeled potatoes from a bushel basket. It was the first time she had spoken while Lee visited.

"Hard," the old woman said. "They knocked me down."

"You didn't know any of them?" Lee asked.

"They were strangers. All strangers."

At supper that night Lee asked whether there was a synagogue in the city.

"A very beautiful synagogue," Dr. Biehl said, and his wife echoed him. "It's gone now, but I remember it."

"Where was it?"

He told her the street. She was sure she had walked there but could not remember anything that might once have been a synagogue.

The next day at lunch she asked Sally.

"I'll take you there," Sally said. "I want to go down that way anyway. Wendy needs some new underwear and there's a little shop near there. Finish your coffee."

57

They went down into the lower city, Sally asking questions about Lee's project.

"I've set aside the folktales for a while. I've suddenly become interested in the war, in what happened to the Jews. From the German point of view."

"Nothing happened from the German point of view," Sally said. "You talk Auschwitz, the Germans talk Dresden."

"I'm not talking Auschwitz. I'm just asking questions of a peasant woman living in a little village that no one could find without a native guide, but American tanks landed there in nineteen forty-five."

"Did she ever hear of Jews there?"

"Oh, yes. She's named some of them for me."

"The next thing is she tells you how she helped save one of them."

"Is that what usually happens?"

"If every German who says he saved a Jew really had, there wouldn't have been a Holocaust."

"The Biehls haven't told me anything like that."

"Maybe the Biehls are honest people," Sally said.

"You're a cynic, Sally. Did Sam ever tell you that?"

"Compared to Sam I'm a lunatic optimist."

Lee sighed. "Poor Wendy."

"Yes, poor Wendy. Well, sweet lady of cheer, here's your synagogue."

They had stopped before a wide vacant lot, muddy in the January rain. Running along the rear was a low, uneven concrete wall that once might have been part of the foundation of a building. At the right end was a bicycle rack with three bicycles in it.

"There's nothing here."

"Right. When the war was over, the Germans took down what was left of it after Kristallnacht to erase an irritating reminder of what 'other' Germans did so long ago. It's all gone now and so are all the people who once worshipped here, and even those who in their last pitiful moments may have wished they worshipped here."

"There isn't even a sign."

"You've noticed."

Lee walked onto the earth. It was slick, covered with ugly, dried vegetation.

"In the spring the weeds will sprout," Sally said. "It gives the place a wonderful green look, you know, like a well-cared-for garden. The weeds were still green when we arrived in the fall."

"You'd think they'd put up some kind of a sign," Lee said. It was so bleak, so gone to ruin.

"They all have their own lives to think about, their hopes and dreams and problems. Why should they worry about putting up a sign commemorating the evil their fathers did? That's a tough thing to acknowledge, you know, that your father committed evil. Where was Dr. Biehl the night they burned the synagogue?"

"I don't know."

Sally looked at her sharply. "Don't worry about it. He was probably in medical school or something. I'm sure he wasn't involved." She smiled quickly.

"I feel very sad here."

"Isn't it a shame that only a Jewish girl from

America feels sad here? Come home with me, Lee. I'll make a pot of cocoa and warm us all up. We can talk to Sam. He'll make us laugh."

Lee swallowed hard. "Wendy needs underwear."

"Wendy can wait. Let her father buy it for her. He can use the exercise."

Chapter Five

After coffee on Friday afternoon Lee walked into the city with Marty to buy things for supper. Even though Frau Biehl had a larger refrigerator, she continued to shop daily, convinced that nothing tasted as good as what you bought fresh.

"I went to the cemetery this morning," Lee said as they headed toward the center of town. "It's very pretty there."

"Mummy picked the spot when Daddy died. She didn't know then that three would be buried there."

"I saw Robert Becker at the house after the funeral. He's the only person I ever drank *Brüderschaft* with. Do you remember?"

"Yes. It was very exciting. He made it so dramatic."

"He still seems like a very nice person."

"He is. He came to visit us when Mummy brought Tina home and gave her a lovely gift. Mummy had been so sick before Tina was born, you know. Well, you don't know because you had

61

left. We were all so happy that she came through it well. Robert offered to drive her places if she needed a ride and Daddy wasn't available. Oh Lee, I wish you weren't here at such a sad time."

"The other times were happy."

"All your visits seem to run together into one big celebration. They were all like a second Christmas."

"They were all a lot of fun for me."

"Lee, when you were here the first time—what is it, twenty, twenty-one years ago?—I've always meant to ask you about this—at the end of the year there was a man."

At the end of the year there was a man. They had begun the climb into the upper part of the city. There was a tug at her calf muscles. "Rich," Lee said.

"Yes, Rich." Marty's face broke into a smile. "Richard, wasn't it?"

"Yes."

"I remember him because he was older, he was—mature. We used to tease Marlies about her 'cavaliers' but hers were boys and your Rich was a man."

"He was, yes."

"You made such a beautiful couple. It was very exciting to me. He brought Mummy flowers once and he was always very kind to me. I thought it must be so wonderful to be as old as you and in love with such a wonderful, handsome man. I remember hoping you would marry him."

Lee laughed. "I remember hoping the same thing."

"Why didn't it happen?"

"He was already married."

"Oh."

She had the feeling of bursting a twelve-year-old's bubble although the woman beside her was thirty-two or thirty-three. "They were separated that year. His wife stayed in the States, while he taught in Frankfurt. He thought the marriage was over, but I think she didn't feel the same way."

"So you went home and married someone else and it wasn't right."

"That's it exactly. I married someone else and it wasn't right."

They walked up past the potter, the optician, the little shop that had a pewter coffee set in the window, up past what had been the Mensa but was no more.

"Since we're talking about people from a long time ago, what ever happened to your parents' friend, Dr. Holz?"

"Oh, they still live in town. Dr. Holz retired from the Bundestag several years ago. He was older than Daddy, you know. I didn't remember that you knew them."

"They came to dinner at your house."

"What did you think of him?"

"Better left unsaid," Lee said. "Isn't that our shop just ahead?"

The Holzes had come to a Sunday dinner at the Biehls' about the time that Lee had begun interviewing Frau Möck about the war. Dr. Norbert Holz — the title, like most such designations in Germany,

63

was a Ph.D.—had just returned from a visit to Japan which he had made as a member of the Bundestag, and the Biehls were anxious to hear his stories of Tokyo and the Japanese.

The sight of Dr. Holz as he entered the living room that Sunday afternoon was a shock. He was a big man, heavy, with a jowly, pockmarked face. His wife, however, was a slim woman who looked neither particularly German nor particularly anything else.

The dinner was a pleasant diversion with stories of Japanese food, traffic, industry, and personalities. Dr. Holz had returned only three days earlier and tomorrow he would go back to Bonn to report on his findings.

Frau Holz, who frequently spent weekends in Bonn with her husband, had decided to visit her daughter in Frankfurt next weekend and said she would be taking the train on Thursday.

"I was planning to go to Frankfurt myself this week," Lee said. "I want to visit the Goethe House. May I offer you a ride?"

"How kind of you, Miss Stein. I'd be delighted. If you could drop me at the main station, my daughter can pick me up in her car. She has a beautiful new BMW."

They made it definite, and Lee picked her up at nine on Thursday morning. It was an easy drive, about thirty kilometers on an ordinary road and then about an hour on the Autobahn.

They chatted about Lee's classes and about Old Peter. Frau Holz told her about her husband's career in the Bundestag. He had been a representative of this area since the fifties, and nowadays there was little serious opposition to him at elections. He was very popular with the voters.

Lee talked a little about the United States, her university years, the skyscrapers in New York. The German word for skyscraper was "cloudscratcher." It made her feel itchy.

"Have you visited America?" she asked as a sign for the first Frankfurt turnoff passed by.

"We wanted to once, in the early fifties, but the Americans wouldn't let my husband in."

"Oh?"

"He was in the SS during the war."

She felt half-choked by the news, by the matter-of-fact way in which it had been delivered. "He was what?" she said, thinking she must surely have misheard, misunderstood, misjudged.

"The SS," Frau Holz repeated. Then, clarifying for her American driver, "Nazi."

"I see."

"Probably they would let us in now, but my husband doesn't want to go. He was quite angry about it."

"Yes," Lee said. "I can see that he would be."

"It was extraordinary," Lee said the next day at lunch with Sally.

"The Goethe House?" Sally said with a wry smile.

"Her admission. Her matter-of-factness. Just blurted it out as though she'd said he was a Democrat or a Republican."

65

"That's what it meant to her. It was an affiliation, one she's probably proud of, but she couldn't gauge your reaction. So she didn't brag."

"I sat at the dinner table with that man, Sally. I listened to him with the kind of respect I would give to an ordinary, decent human being."

"What would you have done if you'd known in advance? Stayed up in your room and gone hungry?"

"I don't know." She had thought about that herself last night, driving back from Frankfurt alone after visiting the Goethe House. "Maybe called you and Sam and invited myself over."

"It would have been our pleasure, Lee."

She was unable to write home about it. She had written long letters about the Biehls, the kitchen-table crowd at Frau Möck's, her many adventures and misadventures. This she could not put down on paper. *I had Sunday dinner with an SS man who is now a respected member of the Bundestag. Later in the week I did his wife the favor of driving her to Frankfurt.* It would upset them too much. They would not be able to show the letter to her grandparents.

A few days later she saw Frau Dierich again in the street. Lee stood at a store window, pretending to look inside as Frau Dierich walked by, carrying a cotton net full of small, wrapped food packages. These two people live in the same city, Lee thought, watching the small departing figure descend the steep street, the hunter and the hunted. Did Frau Dierich know that Dr. Holz was a former SS man? Did she tell her friends not to vote for him? Was she able to believe, all these years after the war, that it was really over?

The street curved and the little woman disappeared.

Frau Möck's reminiscences were golden. She had a wonderful story about Leo, the Jew from another village who had returned from the war. He had been a kind man, she said. When someone was sick, he sent flowers. When hard times fell, a basket of food was left at the door. Leo had survived the war but neither his wife nor his best friend had. He had returned to his little village, not far from here, Frau Möck said, and built himself a fine house, but he was only to live in it two years before cancer took him.

"It was very sad," she said. "Only two years in such a fine house." She looked sad. The sisters-in-law were silent. "Once, when my husband needed new boots, Leo gave him a pair," she said. She sighed.

Lee turned off the tape recorder.

In March and April she traveled through Europe with another American student. She said good-bye to everyone and promised to come back, to continue the work. In the meantime she saw all of Western Europe in her little red car. She returned to a somewhat changed household. Marlies was in love and her parents were less than happy at the development.

67

"She sees too much of him," Frau Biehl told Lee on her first afternoon back. "The smiles, the looks, the hand-holding. Her schoolwork is suffering."

"She'll pull herself together for her exams," Lee said. "She's a very bright girl, Frau Biehl."

"Even bright girls can be affected by men. Haven't you had men friends who took over your whole being?"

Lee smiled. "Yes, I have. It's true."

"This year all you're interested in is tape recording stories."

"Not entirely. I keep my eyes and ears open for the other."

"Good. I'm glad to hear it."

Frau Möck was also concerned that Lee was twenty-two and unmarried. "At your age, I already had a son," she said one afternoon before the tape recorder started to run.

"Are you worried about me?" Lee asked.

"A woman needs a husband. You shouldn't wait too long to find one. You could also run the tape recorder with a husband at home."

"That's true. When I get back to the States, I'll start looking or a good man." Then she turned on the tape recorder and slid comfortably back into the war years.

"Am I the first American you've ever met?" she asked Frau Möck as she gathered her things at the end of the session.

"The first one I've met, yes. But I've eaten one."

Lee looked at Frau Möck's face for an explanation, certain she had misunderstood.

Frau Möck burst into laughter and the sisters-in-law smiled. "I have eaten an American," she repeated with glee.

"I don't understand."

"Bisquick," Frau Möck said. She looked quite merry. "After the war there was Bisquick everywhere. We baked little cakes out of it." She showed the size with her hands. "We called them 'Amis.'" She laughed again, delighted with her guest's confusion. "Ami" was the short form or nickname of *Amerikaner*. "So I never knew an American, but I've eaten one."

"I see." She laughed, sharing the joke.

"You don't use Bisquick at home?"

"Not very much." She remembered a box her mother had bought once, years ago, and thrown out still half full.

"But in Germany after the war, everyone used it."

"Frau Möck, I'll remember you as the only woman I ever met who ate an American."

Frau Möck roared.

"I must talk to you, Lee," Marlies said one bright, warm day in May. "Let's go outside and sit in the sun."

The gardener had spent several days working around the house and from the patio they could see the effects of his labor. They carried two summer chairs outside and sat. The sun warmed them. It had been a long time since the sun's warmth had been noticeable.

"It's beautiful, isn't it?" Marlies said.

"It is, yes. Look at those tulips." There were clusters of red, yellow, and white.

"Lee, it's very serious between Robert and me."

"What do you mean?" She had a sudden awful feeling that Marlies wanted to marry and forget about college. For Robert it would be even worse. He wasn't even twenty.

"I mean we're desperately in love."

"That's wonderful, Marlies."

"It's awful."

"Is something wrong?"

"We're never alone."

"I can see that that would make it difficult."

"I don't know how it is in America, but here we still don't have cars, nobody's parents ever go away, all we do is go to parties where there are twenty people or more and we're *never alone*." She sounded very plaintive.

"Things will be different at the university," Lee said, knowing that was not an answer.

"But we love each other now. I was thinking. Your friends, the Gordons. They go away on weekends sometimes, don't they?"

Oh, God, Lee thought. How am I going to handle this? "I think so, yes," she said aloud.

"If they went away — if there were a time that their apartment were empty — if you could ask them for the key. You could say," she went on hurriedly, making it plain that she had rehearsed this little speech, "that you needed to be away from our family for a little while. You know, perhaps Mummy was getting on your nerves." Marlies laughed nervously. "Could you?" she asked in a small voice. "Would you?"

"I could," she said, wishing she had never agreed to this little tête-à-tête in the May sunshine. "I don't know if they have plans to go away soon. I haven't asked them." She felt quite nervous herself. Frau Biehl would kill her if she found out. It would be a betrayal of their trust. What if . . .

"We only want to sit quietly in an empty room," Marlies said. "We want to be able to talk softly and hear each other. We want to be able to look into each other's hearts." She stopped. "You look very unhappy, Lee."

"I am."

"You think I'm asking for more than I'm really asking for. Please. You've had boyfriends. You know you can't have a real relationship when you're always in a crowd."

"I know." Lee got up and walked away, off the patio and onto the green lawn. This plateau was a piece of the world she would carry home with her in the summer, something forever hers, something more wonderful than anything she had ever experienced and perhaps would ever experience again. Marlies wanted something like that for herself. When they started college, she and Robert might never see each other again. This was, after all, only a high school romance, but perhaps . . . Still, she was scared. That big *what if* loomed in front of her. "I'll try, Marlies," she said, returning to the patio. "I

71

promise. I'll tell Sally I'd like to use her apartment if they go away."

"Thank you, Lee." Marlies smiled her wonderful, warm smile. It was no wonder Robert loved her. She jumped up from her chair and hugged Lee. "You're better than a sister."

"So are you, Marlies. Much better."

She drove to the village knowing that they were near the end of their time together. The stories had become repetitive with little new material. What she had was a picture of a farming village in wartime. Last week Frau Möck had portrayed the arrival of the Americans. It was at that moment that Lee first understood the meaning of unconditional surrender; it meant that there was an American soldier on every square inch of Germany and Germany had no alternative but to lay down its arms.

The townspeople had been terrified of the Negro soldiers. No one in the village had ever seen a black man before. The priest, however, with all his worldly knowledge—in spite of the fact, Frau Möck had explained for her "Protestant" guest, that our priests do not marry—had warned the women to stay away from the Negro soldiers. Negroes were hotblooded, he told them. When once they saw a woman, they could not rest until they had her.

"That's not really true," Lee interjected, feeling her liberal American soul in torment.

"Yes, it is," Frau Möck assured her. "The priest knows."

She let it go, not wanting to upset the balance of their acquaintanceship. Frau Möck continued. The first days after the end of the war. The return of the men. How lucky they were to grow their own food because all over Germany there was hunger except in the farming villages.

"It was good that it was over," she said finally, and Lee had the feeling that it was ending now, these afternoons around the kitchen table, this relationship with Frau Möck and her nameless ever present sisters-in-law and the grandmother who slipped in and out, smiled, and offered greetings.

The tape ran a few seconds, recording silence. "And the people who were taken away," Lee said. She had memorized their names a long time ago: Herr Mandelbaum, Frau Weinberger, Herr Rubenstein, Herr Handelmann, the tailor Herr Frenkel. She had heard Frau Möck say back in January that one of them had come back but she wanted to round out the story of the war. She wanted to hear it again, now in the context of dinner with the SS man, Dr. Holz.

Frau Möck shook her head. The tape was still running. One of the sisters-in-law coughed.

"Gone," Frau Möck said. "They never came back."

"You seem very sad," Lee said. She was sure there was something more but she did not know what to say to bring it forth.

Frau Möck nodded. She looked at her sisters-in-law, then at Lee. "I will tell you one last story," she said. Her ebullient self had evaporated. A different woman sat across the rough wooden table. "You

73

have a good heart. Maybe you can understand. You're young and American and you don't know how it was in those days. Herr Mandelbaum. I knew him. I knew his wife. We baked bread together on the same day. She was good to my children. She went to see a sick cousin in another village. She had to go at night because she was a Jew and her passport was no good. If they picked her up, that was the end. While she was gone, someone heard they were coming for the Jews. I left Oma with the children and put my heavy coat on. It was a cold winter and there was no new fabric to sew with. My coat was old, but still warm. I went to their house and knocked on the door. 'Herr Mandelbaum,' I said when he let me in, 'everyone in the village says they are coming soon for the Jews.'

" 'What can I do?' he asked me. 'My wife is gone. Where can I go? They'll find me wherever I go.'

"He was a small man, Herr Mandelbaum, clean-shaven. It isn't true they all had beards. 'Maybe you can hide,' I told him.

" 'Yes,' he said, 'I will try to hide.' But I could see he was just saying it. 'Thank you for warning me, Frau Möck.'

"I stood at the door about to go. 'What about the boy, Herr Mandelbaum?' I said. He had a boy about five years old. An only child.

" 'Take him for me, Frau Möck,' he said. 'When the war is over, I will come and get him.'

"I was speechless," Frau Möck said. At the table, there wasn't a sound, not a breath. Lee could almost feel a trembling in her fingers. "I couldn't say yes

74

and I couldn't say no. I had a husband and my children and Oma in the house. And the others." She waved a hand toward the end of the table where the silent sisters-in-law sat as though perhaps, they, too, had been part of that extended household. "Herr Mandelbaum left me at the door and went into a bedroom. He was gone a long time. I was frightened. I thought, 'If they come while I'm here, they'll take me away, too.' But nobody came, and after a while, he came back with the boy and a suitcase. He lifted the boy and kissed him. Then he said, 'Be good to Frau Möck. When the war is over, Mama and I will come and get you.'"

"He wanted to help me with the suitcase, but I was afraid. I carried the suitcase and held little Simon's hand. We got home without any problems."

Frau Möck stopped speaking. Lee looked at her. The eyes were far away.

"The next day," she went on, "they came and took Herr Mandelbaum. And the others. Frau Mandelbaum I never saw again either. Maybe they found each other somewhere. Maybe in heaven."

"And the boy," Lee said, "Simon. He stayed with you?"

"Till the end of the war. I took him home and I took all of his little clothes and cut off the star. Every little jacket Frau Mandelbaum had sewed a star on. Wait. I'll show you." She pushed her chair back from the table and went to a shelf in the kitchen. "Here," she said, bringing back a box the size of a cigar box.

In it were photographs, some of which she had

shown Lee months earlier, pictures of village weddings and funerals, a small child dressed in a native costume lying in a small casket. From under the snapshots and papers she pulled out the yellow stars. There were still pieces of dark thread clinging to them.

"My God," Lee said in English. She took one from Frau Möck and held it in her hand.

"You don't know, you didn't live here," Frau Möck said. "They had to wear them when they went outside. That was the law in those days."

"But you cut them off."

"Yes, I cut them off. He never walked on the street again till the war was over. He only went outside behind the house when it was safe." She looked out the kitchen window as though she could see the little boy, as though she could assure his safety. "When people came to the house, he stayed in the cellar. Sometimes when there was trouble in the village at night, I slept in the cellar with him." She was quiet, her eyes far away.

Lee was afraid to prod, afraid to utter a word. The yellow star she had held lay in front of her on the table. What happened? she said in her head.

Frau Möck's heavy breast heaved. "No one betrayed us," she said finally. "Simon lived through the war. Then he went outside into the sunshine. He became healthy again."

"What happened to him?"

"The Americans came and the war was over. The Mandelbaums never came back. A few months later there was a knock on the door. I opened it. A mar-

76

ried couple stood there.

" 'Frau Möck?' the man asked.

" 'Yes,' I said.

" 'I am the cousin of Fritz Mandelbaum. We have come for Simon."

"They came into the house and saw Simon. They hugged him and kissed him and cried over him. They told me to pack his things and then they took him away."

"Just like that?" Lee said. "They walked into your house and took him away?"

"My husband never said good-bye to him." She lifted her apron and pressed it to her eyes. When the apron dropped, her eyes were red and her cheeks wet. "They took him away," she said again. "He was my boy."

"Yes."

"Like my own son."

Lee waited until the tears had stopped. "Do you know who they were?" she asked.

Frau Möck nodded. Before she could stand up, one of the sisters-in-law left the table and came back with an old piece of paper. She set it in front of Lee. It was written in the old, prewar script that was nearly illegible. Frau Möck helped her read it. She copied it in clear block letters in her notebook. Frau Möck read it back with approval. The address was in Brooklyn.

Lee closed the book. "You're a wonderful person, Frau Möck. This story—I'm sorry it had such a sad ending. I want to tell you something. I am a Jew."

"You?"

77

"Yes."

"I thought—"

"I am a Jew."

Frau Möck's face lit up. "Do you know them then?"

"No. I've never heard of them. But I'll try to find them for you."

"Imagine that." Frau Möck turned to the Oma who stood in the doorway to the shed. "The American girl says she is a Jew."

The old woman smiled and said something in the dialect. Then she went over to the table and patted Lee on the shoulder.

She made her good-byes and promised to come back in a few weeks. Frau Möck wrapped up a large piece of the day's buttercream cake and insisted that she take it along. The sisters-in-law smiled and shook her hand. As she left, she kissed Frau Möck on the cheek.

Chapter Six

It was the only tape she ever played for the Biehls. Frau Biehl was very moved. She had lost a child, she said, referring to the one between her daughters; she could understand how the poor woman felt.

"Where does Frau Dierich live?" Lee asked afterward.

"Down in the Königstrasse," Frau Biehl said.

It was a street in the lower part of the city, away from the center. The next morning, she looked up Dierich in the phone book and found the one on Königstrasse. After lunch, she went down the hill from the Mensa and found the house. It was an old house on a street of similar old houses. She rang the bell and waited. Finally she knew what she would say to Frau Dierich. For the first time in her twenty-two years she sensed a bond between herself and another person simply because that person was a Jew. Today she would tell Frau Dierich about Frau Möck, that in a little village only a twenty-minute drive from here there was a woman who had done what every German should have done; she had saved a human life. And if it was hard to accept that an SS man had been rewarded with a seat in the Bundestag, then at least it was a comfort to know that in the same area there was a woman who had foiled that SS at peril to herself and her family.

The door opened and the small, pretty woman stood there. "Yes?" she said.

"Frau Dierich, I'm Lee Stein and I'm living at the Biehls' this year. I'm from the United States."

The woman looked at her as though Lee were selling insurance door to door.

"I'm Jewish, Frau Dierich. I wondered if I could talk to you."

Something flashed across her face and was gone. "I'm quite busy today," she said. She smiled slightly. "I don't have the time."

"Perhaps another day."

"I don't think so. Good day, Fräulein."

Lee moved away as the door closed. She had been stupid or insensitive and she had made a fool of herself. She walked down the Königstrasse toward the center of town, made a few turns and came out at the empty lot that had once been a synagogue. Sally had been right. Weeds were sprouting on the untended ground. The Germans had a wonderful word for weeds; it translated into "un-cabbage." In German horticulture, the world divided into cabbage and un-cabbage.

The bicycle rack was full today. How fortunate for the bicycle riders that there was no temple here.

She started to walk again, finally finding one of the narrow streets that led uphill. She kept going up and up till she reached a corner near the marketplace. From there she made her way to the castle.

It was a beautiful May day and the sun was shining on all the red tile roofs with their many chimneys. She sat and looked down at them. She felt an anguish she had never experienced before. From how many of those houses had a Jew like Frau Dierich been taken away during those terrible years? That poor woman, Lee thought. And now that I feel this immense bond toward her, she feels nothing toward me. I had more success talking with the wife of an SS man.

She thought about it till her head hurt. Perhaps she should have written a polite note first. Perhaps she should have asked permission to speak with her. Perhaps, perhaps. What was clear was that Frau Dierich had no desire to talk to her, not today and not any other day. If there was a bond between Lee Stein and anyone, it was with Frau Möck, and that bond was mutual. Frau Möck had trusted her with the most important fact of her life because she had felt Lee was worthy of the trust.

I won't let her down, Lee thought, rising, brushing off her clothes. It was late. On her way down from the castle, she stopped and bought Marty a sweet at one of the shops near the marketplace. When she got home, she kept the events of the afternoon to herself.

The two husbands were returning on Sunday to collect their wives and sons. On Saturday a kind of restlessness overcame everyone except Frau Biehl. The boys, restricted from their usual fun at their grandmother's house, were anxious to go home. Their mothers had become very polite to each other, a sure sign of their growing antagonism.

Lee broke a roll and spread some soft cheese on it. Marlies was drinking her second cup of breakfast coffee. Marty had left to buy a few things for dinner.

"We haven't had much time to talk," Marlies said. She sat across the table from Lee.

"I've been going off by myself. I'm sorry. I haven't felt very social."

"None of us has. I want to visit the cemetery before I leave. Will you come with me?"

"I'd like to."

"After I do the breakfast dishes."

"OK."

Marie-Luise smiled. "You still say OK like a student."

"Everyone says OK."

"I'm so glad you were able to be here, Lee."

"So am I."

They stopped and bought some flowers on the way. The morning fog had lifted and there were patches of blue. It seemed a shorter distance with Marlies walking beside her.

"Robert Becker came and talked to me at the house on Wednesday."

"Robert, yes." Marlies looked at Lee as they walked. "We were both in love that spring, weren't we?"

"Very much."

"Sometimes I think that was the happiest season of my life." She guided Lee around a corner. "No, that's not true. I was happier when I met Kurt."

"Do you think things will work out with him?"

"No, but I'll keep trying."

"I'm sorry."

"Do you know who Robert married? Maria, a girl from my class. They went to the same university. I never cared for her," she added.

"I still remember the night we drank *Brüderschaft*."

"With your arms linked and Marty standing in the doorway and gaping."

"It was all such a lot of fun."

"And your Rich? You stopped seeing him when you went back."

"Yes."

"Mummy told us about it. She said you wrote to her a lot that year she was so sick before Tina was born."

"I did."

"She didn't give us all the facts, of course. But you had told me that spring that he was married. I was so sure he would leave his wife for you."

"I don't know if he ever left her."

They had entered the cemetery and were nearly at the grave. Marlies stopped when they came to the point where they could first see it.

"It's very pretty," she said, her voice thick.

Lee put an arm around her and held her.

"Mummy should have let her go. So what if she didn't live so long? Didn't she have a right to one wonderful experience as a person? As a woman?"

"Marlies, your mother did what she thought was right."

"She *always* does what she thinks is right. But she was wrong this time and she wouldn't listen. She never

83

listens."

"Forgive her for that. She gave every piece of herself to Tina. If I were sick, I couldn't find anyone as devoted and loving as your mother to take care of me. I learned about love from this family."

Marlies looked at her. There were tears on her cheeks. She went to the gravestone and laid the flowers on the grass. Then she stepped back, crossed herself, bowed her head for a minute, and crossed herself again.

"I'll try," she said.

"Is there trouble between you and Marty?"

"Ah, I can't stand people who are jealous."

"Marty isn't a jealous person. And she seems very happy."

"She's nasty about things that I buy. She tells me everything is too expensive. But the truth is, she wants it for herself."

They stood quietly for a few minutes. Then Marlies turned and they walked out of the cemetery side by side.

They walked home a different way, Lee allowing herself to be guided. They came to a street corner and as they waited for a car to cross the intersection, she looked up at the street sign. It was Königstrasse. She glanced left and right but all the houses looked the same.

"Do you remember Frau Dierich?" she asked.

"Frau Dierich. She was a Jew, wasn't she?"

"Yes. Does she still live in town?"

"I think so. I think they built a big house a few years ago. Ask Mummy. She knows."

"And the son. You knew him from school."

"Only slightly. He married a girl from Frankfurt. They may have gone to Israel, Lee. He became a lawyer, you know. I'm sure Mummy knows what happened to him."

"They used to live in the Königstrasse."

"That isn't such a nice street anymore. The city has changed a lot."

"Everything has."

They stopped and bought some chocolate bars for the boys. Then they went home to wait for dinner.

It took her until the following week to tell Sally Gordon about Frau Möck's story. She had been afraid that Sally would disparage the whole thing as a typical German face-saving fiction. To Lee's relief, and to Sally's credit, she didn't.

"There are people who did those things," Sally said in a low, even tone. "Not enough, but that's not your Frau Möck's fault. I met someone at a conference who'd been hidden out by neighbors. Lived in cellars and ate scraps. But he lived."

"This boy was like her son, Sally. When those people came and took him away, it was as if they were taking her own child. I'm sure they had the best interests of that boy at heart, but they broke hers. She wasn't a sophisticated American who could shout and scream about her rights, and anyway, she had just lived through a time of great repression. So she just let him go. If I could find him . . . He must be in his late twenties or thirty by now. I wonder if he remembers any of it."

"You want to find him," Sally said.

"But it's months before I go home."

"Try the consulate in Frankfurt. Or take another couple of hours and drive to Bonn."

"The embassy. Yes. Sally, you're a genius. They could probably cable New York for me. That's just what I'm going to do. I'll drive to Bonn tomorrow. Want to come?"

"No, thanks. I really have to buckle down. If I don't have coffee with you tomorrow, I may get a whole chapter done."

"A chapter during coffee hour. You are a genius. Thanks, Sally." She hurried back to the Biehls' to type up all the information she had on Simon Mandelbaum.

It was one of the most disappointing days of her life. She got up early and had breakfast with the girls at seven. By seven-thirty she was on the road. There were two ways to get to Bonn: the short, slow way using ordinary, picturesque roads straight across Germany or the long, fast way with the Autobahn. The Autobahn was a more circuitous route but easier to follow and had no speed limit. In either case, it was about three hours. She decided to take the picturesque way in the morning and return with the Autobahn.

The embassy was harder to find than she had thought. It was in Mehlem, a suburb of Bonn. The Rhine snaked around and had a multitude of bridges crossing it. She had to find the right bridge and then the right road and it wasn't easy. It was nearly noon when she arrived.

The woman to whom she told the story was unimpressed. This was not an embassy matter. The embassy had no records about people like Simon Mandelbaum. This was a matter for immigration or a private American agency and if Lee wanted . . .

She argued. She lost. Finally, she went to the ladies' room, happy to find American-style plumbing and good quality toilet paper. When she came out, the woman had gone to lunch. Crossing her fingers, she went to the replacement and tried all over again. To no avail.

She left and drove into Bonn to find a place to eat. She had tried and she had failed. Frau Dierich would not speak to her and the embassy — *her* embassy — would not help her.

After lunch she walked around, sightseeing. But she saw very little. She wanted to *do* something, something for Frau Möck. Late in the afternoon she bought some postcards, found a café, and sat sipping coffee, nibbling at a piece of cake, and writing home. When she was finished, it was nearly seven o'clock and she thought she ought to start back.

She made one stop along the Autobahn for some supper and then kept going. Somewhere around Frankfurt she took the northern route toward Kassel. At Giessen she got off. Another half hour and she would be home. She drove carefully. It was foggy, as usual, and these were old, winding, unlighted roads with one lane in each direction. The Germans drove on them at breakneck speeds, but she didn't have their courage.

It was dark and there was almost no traffic. In a

week or two she would have to go back to the village and tell Frau Möck that she had been unable to move even one tiny step forward toward finding Simon.

She went cautiously around a sharp curve. Down the road, on the opposite side, a car had pulled off the road. Its parking lights were on and a person — probably a man but she wasn't altogether sure — was kneeling beside the rear tire. She braked without thinking and signaled to the right. If she had learned one thing this year, it was that people had to help each other — Germans, Americans, Jews, everybody. She was far from the saint that Frau Möck was but she could offer a fellow driver some assistance. She pulled off the road and turned off the motor.

Chapter Seven

The man looked in her direction. She got out of the car and closed the door. She had dressed for the embassy today, a dark suit and a white blouse. She had worn her flat shoes so that she would not intimidate the ambassador. Ha.

"Can I help you?" she called in perfect German.

"Thank you for stopping. I have a flat tire."

She crossed the road. "I can help you change it," she said, thinking, *There go the stockings, the shoes, the clean hands.*

He gave her an odd look. "Are you American?" he asked in perfect American English.

She laughed. "Yes. How could you tell? I've been polishing my accent for months."

"German girls don't look like that. Like you."

"Oh. Well, I guess German men don't look like you either. Except it's dark and I was expecting you to be German. I kind of wanted to do a favor for a German tonight."

"I'm sorry to disappoint you." He held out his hand. "I'm Richard Singer."

"Hi. Lee Stein."

An almost smile. "It's nice of you to stop."

"Can I help you change the tire?"

"I could change it myself but I don't have a spare."

"My father says it's very dangerous to drive without a spare."

"Your father is right. You can end up at the side of a road in Germany and have to wait for an American to stop for you. You'd be surprised how many Germans passed me by."

"How far are you going?"

"To Frankfurt. I'm teaching at the university this year. On Tuesday nights I do a class on modern European history for the soldiers stationed at Giessen, which is why I'm here. Maybe I can get a room in Giessen for the night and get a new tire tomorrow."

"Do you think my spare would fit your car?"

He looked over at the little Volkswagen. His car was small, too, but some other make. "It might."

"Let's try."

"What will your father say?"

She smiled. "I won't tell him. And he's three thousand miles away." She opened the hood of her car—the trunk was in the front—and waited for him to pull the spare out. He took off his jacket and tie first and tossed them in his car. Crossing the road, he rolled up his shirtsleeves.

"How far do you have to go?" he asked, standing in front of the open trunk.

"About thirty kilometers."

"I'm kind of uneasy about having you drive without a spare."

"I'm not."

"Why?"

90

"I have a relationship with this car. It won't let me down."

He looked at her as though wondering if she was serious or joking. She was serious. She and her car were partners.

"I hope it's a firmer relationship than marriage," he said wryly.

"It is."

He pulled the tire out and carried it across the road. Lee followed with the tool pack. He got his jack out of his car and jacked it up. In ten minutes, the tire was changed. He let the car down and stood back.

"Do you think it's safe?" she asked. The tire was clearly the wrong size and the car dipped.

"I'll take it very slowly." He took his wallet out and pulled out a business card. In the dark, she could not read it. "It has all the information Germans think is important. It stops short of my pedigree. If you have to call, my phone numbers are there. I'll bring a new spare with me tomorrow evening."

"It doesn't have to be new."

He looked down at his hands, which must have been dirty, but it was too dark to see. "I'd like to take you to dinner."

"Thank you."

"Make a reservation at the fanciest place in town."

She laughed. "I'll find something."

He reached into the car and took out a notebook. "Your address, please. And the phone number. Sit in the car with the door open."

She wrote it down, drew a little map, got back out of the car and handed the notebook to him.

"You're just going to let a stranger drive away with

your spare tire," he said.

"Yes."

"Why?"

"I trust you."

"I feel I ought to leave a deposit with you, a piece of my soul or something."

"Please don't."

"Where does all this trust come from?"

"It's a long story."

He walked across the road with her and opened the door of the Volkswagen. "I'll be there at six. Make the reservation for six-thirty."

"Good night."

"Thank you. I really mean that."

"It's nothing. You saved my day."

It was after eleven when she turned the key in the Biehls' door. She bolted the door behind her and left the key on the foyer table. She was rarely out late and when she was, Frau Biehl gave her the key. The house was quiet. She went up the stairs without making a sound. There were no lights. Instead of going to her room, she went to Marie-Luise's and tapped lightly on the door.

"Ja?"

Lee opened the door and stepped in. "Marlies," she whispered.

"Lee. What happened? Mummy was so worried."

"I couldn't call. Marlies, I've met someone."

"A man?" She sat up in bed, excitement in her voice.

"A man. It was dark, but I think he's beautiful. He's not much taller than I."

"It doesn't matter. Does he have a good heart?"

"I think he must. I felt — I felt something wonderful when I talked to him."

Marlies made her sit on the bed and tell the whole story, during which she gasped and scolded — "You could have been killed!" — and finally sighed. "It's going to be a wonderful spring for both of us," she said at the end. "Go to sleep. You don't want rings under your eyes. I'll hurry home from school and help you with your hair and your makeup. Oh Lee, I'm so happy for you."

"You didn't need to buy a new tire. The spare had never been used before."

"I was afraid I'd damaged it irreparably."

They were in the dining room of the old hotel, practically the only diners. In the light of day she could see that she had been right; he was a beautiful man.

"Irreparable damage," she said thoughtfully. "Sounds pretty harsh for a spare tire."

"I wanted to be sure it was safe for you."

"What brought you to Frankfurt?" She had looked at his card in the light of her bedroom last night. Richard Singer, Dr. Phil. Two addresses and two phone numbers.

"I wanted to teach young Germans about the war, club them over the head with it."

"And?"

"I couldn't do it. I teach them, but I don't do any clubbing. They're just kids. They were born after it was over, most of them. I ended up taking a softer approach. I let them do the clubbing. I wrote a word or phrase on a bunch of slips of paper and let them draw. One guy got Auschwitz, one got Eichmann, Malmédy, Dresden.

93

They have to research, write, and deliver a report. It opens eyes."

"I don't think I could listen."

"I've got almost perfect attendance. And an offer to stay on next year."

"Will you?"

"I don't know."

"Are you called Dick?"

"Rich. My mother called me Dicky. I got rid of that as soon as I was old enough."

"Dicky. You don't look like a Dicky."

"And what are you doing here? Besides handing out spare tires at the side of the road."

"I'm on a Fulbright. I came here to collect original, unpublished tales and songs from the folklore. Don't ask me why. I thought it would be fun and in a remote way, sort of scholarly." She sighed and he smiled. "I even got started on it last fall. In a little village about twenty kilometers from here. But then I got an idea and—you must know how these things are if you've done research—it just took me over."

"That's the way the great ideas are."

"You know, being here, being in a place that isn't your country, isn't your language, isn't your culture, the lines aren't drawn as sharply. You can do things you couldn't manage at home. They forgive you little slips. They allow you blunders and discourtesies. You can ask people questions you would ordinarily hesitate to ask strangers and they open up to you."

"Maybe it's you, not the bending of the rules."

"I don't know. All I know is, I plunged in. And nothing has been the same."

"What's different?"

94

"I really love these people. Not just the Biehls, the people in this village. Three women around a kitchen table and an old woman who's always nearby and almost never says anything."

"Are you going to tell me the great idea or do I have to guess it?"

"It's kind of a long story."

"It is, as they say, my nickel."

She told him about Frau Möck, about the first tentative questions and the enthusiastic answers. She found herself translating Frau Möck's strongly accented German quite literally so that he would get the flavor of the narrative. When she got to the finale—"I will tell you one last story"—she could hardly speak. At the end, she was in tears.

He left her at the table dabbing at her eyes with a tissue and settled the bill. When he came back, he said, "Let's go."

"I'm sorry," she said as they walked through the lobby to the street.

"For what?"

"For making a scene."

"That isn't called a scene."

They got into his car and drove to the other side of the city and up the hill. On a quiet road he pulled the car off to the side. It occurred to her that this was what Marlies wanted so much, to be alone with Robert.

"She never saw the child again," Rich said.

"No. When I told her I was Jewish, she asked if I knew his family. They have kind of a primitive view of the world, but she's not dumb. I told her I'd try to find him so I drove to the embassy yesterday—"

"You were coming back from Bonn last night?"

"Yes."

"You're a real go-getter."

"But they treated me like some kind of subversive. They were snooty and curt. What are they there for? I'm a citizen of that country."

"People need green cards. Vice-presidents and their wives come through to make headlines. Senators want permission to buy at the PX."

"No wonder my father complains about his taxes." She laughed.

"You're very pretty."

She wanted to touch him. She had gone out with a few Germans during the year, to parties mostly. But although her German was quite good and the young men had done their best to make her enjoy herself, she had missed something that she could only identify as American. Whatever it was, Rich had it.

"When I saw you at the side of the road last night," she said, "I thought, I am going to stop and help this poor German whose car has broken down, so that I can pay back Frau Möck in some tiny way for doing what she did."

"You don't owe her anything, the Germans do. People like her save them from collective failure. When you get back to the States, I'll get you some addresses in New York, people who'll help you find the boy."

"He's not a boy any more. He must be about your age."

"I'm thirty."

She sat looking out the window. It had grown dark since they left the hotel. *I'm thirty.* It had been a strangely intimate statement, as though he were telling her something he knew she wanted to know but wouldn't ask. *I'm thirty* and whatever else you want to know about me I'll tell you.

"Want to take a walk?"

"Yes."

They got out of the car and walked up the road. They had parked in a clearing, a meadow. Up ahead, where the hill crested, the forest began and the road seemed to cut a strip through it.

"It's a beautiful country," she said.

"It is."

"I came here to have a good time, you know, the last, big good time before the moment of truth. I thought when it was over, I'd go home and get a job. Do the honorable thing, as my father says, earn a living. And watch it all become a memory."

"And now?"

"Everything's different now. I'll never really leave it behind. This town owns a part of me. And that village."

"Isn't that preferable to having a good time and leaving it all behind?"

"Yes. Much. But it hurts."

He ruffled her hair. Marlies had brushed it to perfection in the minutes before his arrival. She would be happy to see it ruffled.

"I'm married," he said.

She stopped walking and turned to face him. In the dark he was little more than an outline. "Couldn't you have told me that before I fell in love with you?"

He put his arms around her and held her without kissing her. She had said it as a joke but now, feeling him against her, she knew it was true. *Dear Mom, I met someone at the side of the road and I fell in love with him the next night, and he's married.*

He released her, put an arm around her, and they kept walking. "My marriage is not as solid a relationship as you have with your car. We aren't living together. She's in Boston and I'm in Frankfurt. We planned it that way. It hasn't been a very good marriage."

"Thank you for telling me. I'm sure the embassy wouldn't have been very helpful if I'd gone to inquire."

This time he kissed her. This time he touched her body in a way she had not let any of the German suitors even think of doing. This time she thought she sensed a beginning.

"That's a nice family you live with," he said when they were walking again. "They care about you."

"I was very lucky. One of Marie-Luise's teachers asked if they'd like to have an American student and her parents said yes. They got me, I got them."

"Says something for arranged marriages, doesn't it?"

A car came toward them, its lights bright, its motor straining.

"What makes a marriage go wrong?" she asked.

"Do you mean *a* marriage or my marriage?"

"Both, I suppose. Your marriage."

"What went wrong was that it didn't go right. We didn't rush home to see each other every night. I had people I talked to and she had people she talked to, and we never seemed to talk to each other. We were faithful to each other in the physical sense — at least I was — but there was nothing before and after. If you know what I mean. You probably don't."

"I've seen marriages like that and they stay together. For years."

"I don't want to live that way. I don't think she does either. When the Frankfurt job came through, she seemed relieved that there was a good excuse for being apart. It was like a catalyst. It made things happen that hadn't happened before because there was no need for them to happen. We started talking about what was wrong when we'd never admitted, at least to each other, that something was."

"You sound very analytical."

"I've given it a lot of thought. I think that's a sign of how bad things were. I'm not a hopeless romantic, but I like the feeling of doing something because I want to do it, not because it's right or expedient or, as the Germans always say, *gesund.*"

"They do worry about things being healthy, don't they?" Washing in cold water was healthy; drinking cold water was not; walking up a steep street was healthy; eating — God help her — *Schmalz* spread on rye bread was healthy. The thought of it made her feel like choking.

"I can't think of anything healthier than being here right now."

"If Frau Möck hadn't told me that story, I wouldn't have stopped last night."

"Yes you would."

"You don't know me that well."

"You're affected by people in distress. You saw someone who needed help and you acted. You didn't pass by, think about it, and back up. You ought to be careful though. You're very pretty, and a man at the side of the road can be trouble." He walked closer to the edge of the road and looked at his watch. The moon was just over the road, pouring light onto the strip between the two halves of the forest. "I'd better get you home."

They turned and started back. "You said you didn't want to live that way," she said. "How do you want to live?"

"I want to feel things. I feel things in that class I'm teaching, the one in Frankfurt. The soldiers in Giessen — they're a little too on edge to be very inspirational. There's one captain in the class, and even though most of them show up out of uniform and I call them all Mr., his presence is intimidating. But he's the most interesting person in the class."

"I miss American classes. No one ever speaks up here. Except me. And it's been a bit awkward sometimes. The professor thinks I'm challenging his authority."

"Are you?" He sounded amused.

"Not usually."

"Imagine challenging authority." He pulled her closer and kissed her cheek. "Clear sky, isn't it? You can pick out the constellations. In Boston you can hardly find a star."

"Do they challenge yours?"

"Not as much as they should. I try to leave myself open to it, but usually they don't bite. It's an interestingly different mentality."

"Maybe it's just a different style, a different set of conventions, like cutting sandwiches with a knife and fork instead of lifting them with your hands."

"Possibly."

"Because when you get down to rock bottom, their feelings are just the same as ours. That woman in the village had her child taken from her and she will hurt forever. Frau Biehl gave birth prematurely and the baby died and she will never forget it."

"Write a paper about it."

"I might. I'll talk to my friend Sally. She's a sociologist."

"What are you?" The car was up ahead, sitting in the moonlight.

She thought of answers: happy, content, alive, excited. "No label yet," she said.

"Will you come down to Frankfurt for the weekend?" They had stopped in front of the car. It was so light she could see him clearly.

"Yes."

"I'll get you a hotel room. You can tell Frau Biehl it's quite safe."

"I think she's clever enough not to ask."

He touched her face with a finger. "I'll get one anyway."

He kissed her, forestalling their departure and opening a chasm of need. He would be a good man to fall in love with, a good man to be close to. They walked around to the passenger side and he let her in. When he was behind the wheel, he held his keys in his hand for a minute. "I talked a lot tonight," he said.

"It was nice to hear English. It was nice to hear you."

"And you."

The tension in the car seemed almost visible, something bright pulsing between them. They sat in their separate seats with the emergency brake and gear shift creating a barrier between them.

"It's been a different kind of year for me," he said. "I've spent most of my waking hours working on my Frankfurt classes. My German isn't what it should be and I want to speak it well as a matter of pride. The old couple downstairs have helped me phrase things, and we've thrashed out a lot of the stuff I talk about in class. He's a retired teacher and he's been very helpful." He paused. "I'm trying to say something and I'm not doing very well."

"Maybe you don't have to say it."

"I took on the Giessen job to give myself more to do and keep my free time down to almost nothing. It's easier to say you're busy when you're busy. I've been trying to resolve my marriage by being reclusive. The truth of my marriage is that we haven't written to each other for three or four months, and I don't hurry home to check the mail."

"You don't owe me an explanation of your marriage."

"Maybe what I'm trying to say is that I don't feel married and that's why I asked you down to Frankfurt this weekend."

"I accepted."

"You know that if we see each other, if we keep seeing each other, we'll end up in bed one day."

She didn't say anything.

"It's not a threat and not a promise. It's just the way things are."

She turned to look at him. His face was blanched in the moonlight that poured through the windshield. "Why were you driving without a spare last night?"

He seemed momentarily startled by the question. "Can you think of a better way to meet an American girl who cares about the less fortunate?"

Chapter Eight

Kurt was the first of the husbands to arrive on Sunday. They had finished breakfast and Marlies was packed and ready, her boys out on the grass when their father arrived. He was polite and friendly, agreeable to a short visit before leaving for home with his family.

Lee watched him, watched them together. There was no indication that his wife was not the most important person in his life, that he did not have great feelings of fondness for his mother-in-law. Who can tell? she thought. Maybe whatever it is will blow over and they'll find themselves in love again. Hopeless romantic. Rich had used the phrase once, denying he was one.

How much times had changed. Twenty years ago you could go out with someone and still feel that sex was a choice, not a necessity, the way it had been for Marlies and Robert—if it had been that way for them after all. Today it was only the fear of disease that kept sex from being inevitable, even in casual relationships.

"Where's Marty?" Marlies asked, bringing Lee back from her daydreams. In the twenty years since she had left, she had visited this country, this house, many times but she had refused, by an act of will, to think of Rich. Now that she had allowed it, invited it, memories poured in. Everything made her think of him: this living room, that patio, the looks that Marlies and Kurt gave each other. He had filled her life in those last months — "Lee? Have you seen Marty?"

"Not since breakfast. I'll look upstairs."

"Stay here. I'll go." She left the room.

"I hope you'll visit us on your next trip," Kurt said. He sounded sincere. He hadn't had to say it. He could have commented on the weather or the newspaper headlines or the smell of dinner cooking. "We'll all be in better humor next time you come."

"Thank you. I will, Kurt. And there's room for two in my apartment. Just let me know when." They had never visited her, never visited the States despite many invitations.

Marlies came back. "She's gone. She must have left the house." She looked distressed. "I won't get to say good-bye to her."

"We really should leave," Kurt said.

When they had said good-bye to Frau Biehl in the house, Lee accompanied them to the bottom of the stairs where the Mercedes was parked. Marlies took Lee's hand and walked a little way down the street with her.

"I feel it just now for the first time," she said. "I will never come home again and find Tina here." She started to cry. "Please write to me, Lee."

"I will."

"Not just to Mummy. To me."

"I will."

"I feel ill." She looked very pale.

"Come sit in the car."

They walked back to the car and Kurt opened the front door. One of the boys started to ask Marlies something but Kurt said, "Leave Mummy alone."

"I'm all right," Marlies said. She had sat down and color was returning to her cheeks. "Good-bye, Lee." They kissed.

"I'll write." She threw a kiss to the boys in the backseat. "Good-bye, Kurt," she said, shaking his hand and kissing his cheek. She stood watching the car as it went down the street. Then she climbed the hundred steps to the house.

His directions had been perfect. She pulled up in front of the house at about eleven Saturday morning. As she turned the motor off, he started down a long flight of stairs that ran along the outside of the house from the top floor, a flight that had probably been added long after the house was built.

She got out of the car and waved, waiting for him. He was wearing jeans and a short-sleeved shirt and looked very American, very appealing. He kissed her lightly on the lips when he reached the street.

"Good trip?"

"Fine."

"Want to walk? Go to the hotel? Wash up?"

"Walk. Shake out the limbs. It's very pretty here."

"It's a nice old quarter." His house was on Beethovenstrasse. Driving the last few blocks, she had passed other composers' names on street signs. "It took a hit during the war. Over there. Down the street."

She could see it as they walked, a bombed-out church on a small square set between two streets, the cause an errant bomb, no doubt, that had found an unintended and undeserving mark. They crossed the street and walked around the ruin with its hollow windows. A street sign said Beethovenplatz. Inside the shell, weeds grew and the sun shone through the roofless top of the building.

"They've left some of these as remembrances of things past. Have you seen the one in Berlin? The Gedächtniskirche?"

"I visited there, yes. It's overpowering. You see it from everywhere. You turn around, almost anywhere, and there it is in the distance. This one's like a hidden secret."

"This country's full of hidden secrets."

"Every country is, Rich."

He took her hand and they kept walking. "I'm glad you're here," he said. "I was more impatient for your arrival than I thought I would be."

As she had been, on the trip down. "I'd like to see where you teach."

"I'll take you over after lunch." They crossed a street. "Then we'll check you into the hotel. Then I'll show you some parts of Frankfurt I think you'll like. Then we'll have dinner . . ." He said it in an unhurried way, outlining the day of pleasure stretched out before them.

"It sounds like the nicest day of the year."

"I hope it will be."

It was. A collection of vignettes that she would never forget: lunch in an outdoor café where she drank Berlinerweisse, pale beer in a huge glass shaped like an oversized champagne saucer and flavored with raspberry juice; a walk along the Main; a drink in the Rathaus square where Justice held her scales without benefit of blindfold; dinner in a dimly lit old restaurant.

They walked out into the dark street touching. They drove touching. He stopped the car in front of his house, and they made the long climb up the exterior stairs holding hands. Inside the door he held her and kissed her. For the first time since she had arrived, she felt again the unreality, the fantasy of being far from home, away, distanced, unencumbered by rules and regulations.

"Let me turn a light on," he said, moving away from her. The apartment was two rooms, a sort of bedroom, a sort of living room with a tiny kitchen built in at one end, and a bath, all of which must once have been an attic. He turned a lamp on in each room and showed her around. Oddly, the door to the outside was in the bedroom.

"I like it."

There were books on shelves lining the living room, and a desk and more books in the bedroom. On the desk several heavy books were open, one on top of the other, left and right of a pad of paper.

"Not as elegant as where you live."

"But more your own." She walked to the desk. "You were working when I got here this morning."

"Just preparing for next week's classes."

"You must spend a lot of time alone, sitting and reading and thinking. Do you like that?"

"It seems to suit me. The way going out with a tape recorder seems to suit you."

"I never thought of it that way, as something that suits me. It was just something I did that seemed the right thing to do at the moment."

"I hope you always do that—what you think is right at the moment." He was standing near the door to the living room.

"I hope so, too."

"Let me get you back to the hotel."

They drove back and he left her. She stayed awake for a long time, thinking of the day they had shared, the places they had seen—the room at the university where he taught, not unlike other classrooms but special to her be-

107

cause it was his — the things they had said to each other. Doing what was right at the moment. He was right. They were right. Everything that had happened was right. She slept well.

Marty came back before one, which was dinner time. She had been at the cemetery. She looked tired but she moved with her usual agility. Her mother had set the table. Marty went to the kitchen and prepared the gravy for the meat. Lee went in to help her carry platters to the table.

"You won't leave too soon," Marty said.

"I'll stay another few days."

"Good. She's not ready to be alone yet."

"Marlies was sorry to miss you."

"Yes."

"She looked all over the house for you."

"I wanted to be alone. I didn't even tell Gerd where I was going."

Her husband, Gunther, arrived at three. Frau Biehl was still sleeping. There were some difficult moments when they were ready to leave and Marty's mother was not yet awake. Frau Biehl had said earler that three was an awkward time to arrive. But quite suddenly, she appeared in the living room, fully dressed and smiling. Marty seemed relieved. Mother and daughter said tearful farewells. Lee slipped out the front door. The weather, at least, was holding.

The departing family came outside a few minutes later. Marty looked done in. She took Lee's hand and held it, saying nothing.

"We may be in the States next year," Gunther said.

"Really?"

"My company is expanding its markets. We would certainly be in New York a few days if we go."

"Please stay with me. You know how much I'd like that."

"We'll write to you, Lee." He picked up the suitcases and started down the stairs. Young Gerd followed.

"I didn't mean to miss Marlies," Marty said. "She never said when Kurt was coming."

"Don't worry about it. Have a safe trip home."

"Mummy is angry that Gunther came at three instead of two or four. He couldn't leave any earlier."

"Your mother wants the world to be different. Everything that's less than perfect adds to her unhappiness. She'll be better in a few months."

"We'll never be better."

"Don't say that."

They said their good-byes and Lee watched her go down the stairs to the street. Then she went inside to Frau Biehl.

"We did a lot of talking over coffee in those days, didn't we?" Frau Biehl said. She had poured the coffee and passed a fruit torte and a plate of whipped cream.

"They were some of the best hours I spent in this house, in this country."

"We didn't always agree."

"We didn't have to."

"With your daughters, you agree or you disagree. If you disagree, there's trouble."

"That's the way it is with mothers and daughters."

"I have something to give you, Lee. I've saved your letters. They're in a box in my husband's study. I'm not going to live forever. I think you should take them."

"You're only twenty years older than I. You have a long time to live."

"Perhaps. It's no matter. The letters are yours. You wrote them. I don't want other people reading them. I'll leave them in your room."

"Thank you."

"Since you're not my daughter, I want to offer you some advice. It gives me pleasure to know that you'll listen to me, even if you don't accept it."

"I'll certainly listen."

"You met a man when you were here twenty years ago. That man meant more to you than the man you later married. The time has come for you to find him. Maybe he's still married to that woman and has forgotten your name. I don't think so. I don't think he's married to her and I don't think he's forgotten you. The mind holds twenty years; it doesn't hold thirty or forty the same way. Do it now, when you get back to New York."

"It isn't easy to find people in the States. We aren't all registered with the police."

"You're a smart woman. You can find him."

"Yes." She looked out the window. The sky was clouding over. April's sun was all but gone.

"You were going to find the little Jewish boy when you left here that time. You didn't do it, did you?"

"No."

"You don't have to explain it to me and you shouldn't blame yourself. When you left here, you were in turmoil. I feared for you. I wanted you to stay."

"I couldn't."

"I know. But those things you never did, they still make

110

you unhappy." It was not a question.

Lee nodded.

"This is an unhappy time for all of us. I am in my sixties now, but you are a young woman. You must go forward."

"I'm going to try."

"I am releasing you from your promise."

She looked at Frau Biehl. She had a structure of cast iron and the sensitivity of a saint. It was quite a combination. Knowing this woman was unlike any other relationship Lee had ever had. Frau Biehl was neither mother nor friend nor sister.

Frau Biehl was right. She had left in turmoil, everything unfinished. Tomorrow she would begin to set things straight.

Lee took a breath. "Marlies said Frau Dierich still lived in town. Do you know where?"

"Yes, of course I know where. Her husband made a lot of money and they built a huge house on the other side of our hill. If you walk there, it will take at least twenty minutes, maybe longer."

"Can you tell me how to go?"

Frau Biehl smiled. "It's very easy. I know the way exactly."

"Will you meet me Tuesday in Giessen for coffee after my class?" It was Sunday afternoon and she was ready to leave. They stood on the street near her red car, saying the kinds of things that prolong a parting.

"Can I sit in on your class?"

He shook his head. "You'll make me nervous."

She laughed.

"I'm serious. Meet me afterward. At the caserne."

111

* * *

Sally had stopped lingering for coffee. They lunched together and then she hurried off to her work.

"So you had a great weekend," she said, picking up a piece of meat and carefully avoiding the grease. "I'm glad to hear someone did. I worked my head off."

"But you're making progress."

"Progress, yes, but I don't think I'll finish. There's still too damn much I don't have."

"What will you do?"

"I don't know." Sally shrugged. "But we're going to Göttingen for the weekend. Sam and Wendy are getting antsy sitting around, and I've got an appointment with a professor there I've been trying to see for months."

"When are you leaving?"

"Friday morning so I can see him in the afternoon. Then we'll make some side trips."

"Sally." Her heart was doing funny things.

Sally looked at her, that wry smile almost breaking.

"If Rich came up this weekend, could he stay at your place? Save a hotel bill?"

It became a smile. "Sure he can."

"Thanks, Sally."

"Come over early Friday and I'll give you my key. Just one thing. I hate to say this, but laundry's so damned expensive. Could you take care of the sheets?"

"Of course I can."

"I hate to ask —"

"Sally, don't apologize."

"It's not very hospitable of me."

"Sally, it's *OK*."

Sally patted her mouth with the thin half-napkin the

112

Mensa dispensed. "The key's yours then." She stared at her plate, staring at nothing.

"Is something wrong?" Lee asked.

Sally met her eyes. "Yes, but it has nothing to do with anything we've been discussing." She pushed her chair back. "Must go. See you tomorrow."

She met Rich Tuesday night and told him about the Gordons' apartment. He said he would drive up Saturday morning.

"How's your intimidating captain?" she asked.

"I hate to say he's smarter than all the enlisted men put together, but it's true. He started out in the Korean War and now he's got a desk job and not long to go for retirement. I'll bring him along next week. You'll like him."

The next afternoon she told Marlies that the Gordons' apartment would be free on Friday night. That evening, the phone rang for Marlies. She answered and spoke for a few minutes, then went to ask her parents for permission to see a movie with Robert on Friday night. Lee sat in the living room listening to the carefully worked-out charade. Dr. Biehl said Marlies would have to be home by eleven but then relented and agreed to midnight. When she hung up, Marlies went upstairs without stopping in the living room, just as if it had been an ordinary conversation with an ordinary invitation.

Lee went to Marlies's room later on. Marlies glowed.

"You see? It worked perfectly."

"I'm very nervous. If your mother finds out, she'll throw me out of the house."

"No one will ever know. Even you will never know, Lee. You'll give me the key but you won't know if I use it."

"OK."

"Right." She smiled broadly. *"OK."*

She gave the key to Marlies after school on Friday. Marlies squeezed her hand as she accepted it. She ate supper early by herself and Robert called for her at seven. Marty went downstairs to see them off, but Lee stayed up in her room till they were gone. Then she went down for supper with the family.

After she had put down the book she was reading and turned off the light, she lay awake listening for the downstairs door. This must be how a mother feels, she thought, when her beautiful daughter goes out for the evening with a handsome boy and their feelings for each other are as apparent as their sexes.

If they had been the same age, she would have given the key without hesitation. But Marlies was three years younger; she was high school, not college; she lived at home, not on her own.

I shouldn't have done it, she thought. I am at fault if anything happens.

The downstairs door opened and shut. She heard small noises on the stairs, the treads responding to a weight. Then her door opened and something was placed on the night table.

"Schönen Dank," a whispered voice said.

Then the door closed.

114

Chapter Nine

Rich arrived before dinner and Frau Biehl insisted they sit on the patio and enjoy the sun. Dr. Biehl arrived soon after, greeted Rich with enthusiasm, offered aperitifs, and began a conversation that lasted for hours. The doctor was interested in Rich's opinion of the threat from the East. It had been a mistake, he said, for the United States, in the last weeks of the war, not to round up what was left of the German forces and rid the world forever of the Communist menace.

The discussion went on through dinner. Frau Biehl excused herself to take her nap and the sisters did the dishes. Lee, Rich, and the doctor exchanged their dinner chairs for patio chairs and the conversation went on, questions, thoughtful answers, disputatious responses.

Suddenly, a huge shadow the shape of a model airplane darted across the garden, mounted the side of the house, whipped across the roof, and was gone.

"Ah," the doctor said, looking up, "the gliders have started."

Moving from right to left over the river was a silent craft. Lee sprang up and walked to the edge of the garden. The glider continued till it was almost out of sight, then turned gently. The shadow had been a foreshadow. "It's wonderful," she said. She stood at the stone wall, watching, while the doctor resumed his questions and Rich, in a curiously gentle way, continued his answers.

"He was in the Soviet Union," Rich said.

They had taken their leave, finally, after coffee and cake and earnest invitations to stay, to return, to keep coming back.

"We've talked about it. His descriptions were very vivid."

"He nearly reached Moscow. It was the snow, in the end, that was their undoing, not the mighty Russian army."

"And typhus. He said the Russians were practically immune. They lived with fleas. The Germans died from them."

"It's an odd feeling to sit down with the enemy and know he's your friend, to be satisfied that he never reached Moscow and to feel for his pain in what must have been the worst winter of his life."

"That's the building." She pointed across the street to where the Gordons lived, and he swung the car around and parked in front.

He looked at his watch. "I wanted to see your little village this afternoon and that ruin you told me about, but the day's almost over."

"It wasn't wasted," she said, almost as a question.

"Nothing's been wasted." He turned off the motor. "I see why you let me go off with your spare. They're very nice people. They would chip away at anyone's cynicism."

The apartment looked exactly as it had on Friday morning when she went to pick up the key. If Marlies had

116

been there last night with Robert, she had not left a trace. Perhaps she had even straightened up a bit after the casual Gordons.

It was a small apartment with few modern conveniences. Although it had been built after the war, it was heated by a single large coal stove in the corner of the small living room. Beside the stove was a bucket of briquettes. There was one bedroom large enough for a double bed and some additional furniture, and a tiny bedroom with room only for Wendy's bed and a small three-drawer dresser. The kitchen was adequate but would fulfill no one's dream. Overall the apartment was drab, but the Gordons seemed happy to have something big enough for the three of them.

Rich closed the door and put his bag on the floor. He had taken his jacket off as soon as they left the Biehls'. It was an unusually warm day, warm in temperature, warm in hospitality.

"They must have had a rough winter," he said, looking at the stove. "Heating this place that way."

"They did, but Sally's a very positive person. After a cold night, she looks for sunshine."

"That sounds like something you would say. Did I tell you I'm glad I'm here?"

"I guessed." Then she did something she had never done before; she unbuttoned her blouse.

He watched until she reached the fourth button. Then he came over and put his hands over hers. He kissed her, still holding her hands. "I would like the pleasure of doing that," he said.

It was a brilliant memory, the memory of that first love.

117

When she thought of that afternoon, that spring, of Rich, she heard the music of the times, the sweet songs that still stirred her, softened her. Often after that weekend she would call him from the post office on her way to class in the morning. Often he would call in the evening from his apartment. Nothing that they said to each other was memorable, but she remembered sitting in the booth at the post office and standing at the downstairs phone at the Biehls'. She remembered feeling happy to hear his voice.

They spent weekends together. She stayed with him in Frankfurt, cooking in his tiny kitchen, eating on a small table in the living room, sleeping on a bed that hardly seemed big enough for one but sufficed for two.

On a Saturday in July Marlies gave her a spray of jasmine to take along, the flower of love. She dropped it on the car seat with her handbag. The perfume scented the car. In Frankfurt she put them in water, hoping they would revive.

Rich opened a bottle of beer and poured two glasses. "I have to make a decision," he said. "They want me to stay on and I think I'd like to, for one more year. If I do, would you stay, too?" He touched her hand. "Don't answer me yet. I know it's too late for you to renew. It would mean your living here. With me. It's the only way I could afford it."

"It's the only way I would do it."

"I like coming home to you," he said.

It was one of the things she wanted to hear. Later, there would be other things, even better than that.

The walk to the Dierich house was longer than she had estimated. On a map it was not far, but on foot it necessitated circling the hill that the Biehl house was on. The route was a wide circle but a pleasant walk. The house was imposing and large. She could not imagine why two people with one grown son would want to live in so large a place.

She walked up the drive to the front door and rang the bell. A dog barked. A woman's voice said something unintelligible. The door opened.

"Frau Dierich."

"Yes." She looked exactly the same but her hair was completely white.

"My name was Lee Stein. I came to see you once—"

"Yes. You were the American Jewess who lived with the Biehls. I was very rude to you."

"No. It was impolite of me to visit you the way I did. I've come to apologize. I'm sorry it's taken me twenty years to do it."

"Not at all," the little woman said with spirit. "It is I who must apologize to you, Miss—"

"Mrs. Linden."

"Mrs. Linden. I was just about to have a cup of coffee. Will you join me?"

"With pleasure."

Frau Dierich seemed very excited. "Just come this way. I'll grind some more coffee. It won't take a minute."

Lee closed the door and followed her down the hallway.

"You never told me," Frau Biehl said at the supper table.

"I was so embarrassed. I don't know what I expected but I certainly didn't expect to be turned down so completely. Nor did I expect to be invited in today with such enthusiasm."

"She's a nice woman. Does her son live in Israel?"

"Yes, with five children! That's why they built the big house. Her son's family visits every year and she wants them to feel at home. Her son became an observant Jew and it changed her. Twenty years ago she couldn't talk about what happened during the war."

"Did she talk about it today?"

"No. I didn't go there for that. But when I told her that time that I was Jewish, she thought I wanted to ask about it. She said she was afraid."

"Poor thing."

"She feels quite different now. She was very kind to me. She admires you, Frau Biehl. You ought to call her sometime and invite her for coffee."

"It's a long walk," Frau Biehl said.

"She drives." Lee felt a moment of triumph. "She learned how to drive and her husband bought her a car."

Part Two

Chapter One

Lee had left Frau Biehl on Wednesday, a week after her arrival, and taken the train to Frankfurt. There she had checked into a hotel and rented a car for the day.

After twenty years it had not been easy to find her way around but with the help of the rental clerk and a good street map, she drove to Beethovenstrasse. The house was still there, the long outdoor flight of stairs still leading to the door on the third floor.

She left the car and walked down to the ruined church. It was no longer a ruin. Glass filled its windows. A roof kept out the weather. A studenty person walked in and an old man came out. The building had been completely restored to its original image and was a kind of interfaith center. Lee felt depressed. Except for the church, time had stood still in this little neighborhood. In the distance there were tall buildings, but here the old enclave had held back an uncomfortable march of progress.

During the afternoon she made a sentimental tour of Frankfurt. She had once told Rich it was a city that tried to be New York; now she felt just the opposite. New York was trying to be Frankfurt. She hoped it would fail. It was only the pockets of old that retained any charm, any appeal. She found a building at the university that looked familiar and walked through it, but she was unable to find the room he had taught in. She was unsure of the floor, of the building itself. Frau Biehl was right. Twenty years was the edge. After twenty you could count on nothing.

"Now or never," she said aloud, hearing a faint echo in the hall.

She drove to the Rathaus square and parked the car in a garage. Idiot, she chided herself. You should have taken taxis.

It was too cold to sit outside but she walked by Justice, unblindfolded, and made her way to a café where she drank a glass of Berlinerweisse and fended off a man who wanted to pick her up. At least I still attract them, she thought, savoring the taste of the sweet beer. What had Marty said? Buy some German filter papers and your coffee will be so good you'll get yourself another husband.

Laughing at herself, she found a little shop and bought a box of forty. If forty cups of coffee didn't do the trick, nothing would. The next day she flew home.

On Friday she went into the office and made an appointment to see the senior partner, Calvin Crain, at ten-thirty. She and Cal had owned a recording company for nearly fifteen years and recently they had branched out into video. Her then fiancé, Ted Linden, had known Cal and the three of them had started a business together. Either the business had interfered with the marriage or the other way around, and Ted had left the company. Later, of course, he had left the marriage, too, for other reasons. She had remained the lesser partner to avoid the problems of inevitable disagreements and the arrangement had worked out well. There had been moments — times — of sexual tension between her and Cal, but over the years, they had achieved a comfortable equilibrium.

"How's ten forty-five?" Lisa, the secretary, said, poking

her head into Lee's office. "The guy he's talking to shows no signs of removing himself."

"Just so long as it doesn't get to be four forty-five."

"Promise."

Lisa was a sweet kid of about twenty-one, the twenty-second secretary they had had in almost fifteen years. It had been an interesting — and demoralizing — progression. The secretaries got increasingly younger and less productive, were paid more and stayed for a shorter period. Recently, there had been several a year, so that on a Monday morning you sometimes had to wonder if you had been introduced.

She got to see Cal a little before eleven.

"How are you?" he said.

"I had a good night's sleep. I'm fine."

"Lisa said you went to a funeral. Was it family?"

"Good friends. The ones I lived with twenty years ago in Germany."

"I'm glad you're back. We've got a lot of things—"

She held up her hand. "I need some more time, Cal. I know how tough it'll be on you but I have to put some pieces of my life in place."

He looked at her without responding. He was a very tall, very thin man, much like her in structure. She had told him during one of their moments that he needed a rounder woman.

"I didn't know your life was falling apart."

"It isn't. I made some promises a long time ago and I didn't keep them. This trip to Germany — there are things I have to take care of."

"We can't afford a mid-life crisis, Lee."

"You won't get one."

"How much time?" he asked flatly, getting down to business as she had known he would.

"If I'm lucky a week. It could be more. It could be a month. It's hard for me to say. If I'm around the city, I'll be in and working."

"What can I say?" he smiled. He was a nice man and she had always liked working with him.

"How about 'Go in good health'?"

"So be it."

On the way back to her office, she swiped the Brooklyn telephone book from Lisa's cabinet. Lisa was typing an envelope. When she finished, Lee said, "When you have a minute, make a phone call for me to Boston University. I want information on Dr. Richard Singer. He taught there in the early-to-mid-sixties. If he's still there, get me his extension. If he's not, see if you can get me a current address, phone number, whatever."

"Richard Singer."

"Yes. I don't know what his title was but he was in the history department. And Lisa, please keep a record of these calls. Cal goes a little crazy over the phone bill. I'll write a check for these."

"Want to talk to him if he's there?"

"No." She was surprised at how quickly she answered, how violently her body reacted. "Just a phone number. I'll call back when I'm not so busy."

She sank into her desk chair feeling panic. Half of her hoped she would never find him. The distance from Germany, from Frau Biehl, the normalcy of New York, of the apartment, the office, the crowds in the street, had widened the metaphorical distance. Keeping Rich a memory was comfortable; seeing him, confronting him, engendered panic.

She took a slip of paper out of her bag and unfolded it on the desk. It had taken no time at all after her return yesterday afternoon to locate the notebook from her work with Frau Möck. In large, clear letters on a date in May was the name of the cousin who had taken Simon Mandelbaum: Murray Greenwald. The address was East Eighteenth Street in Brooklyn. The telephone number started with ES. She had no idea what ES might stand for. Before she dialed, she looked up Murray Greenwald in the Brooklyn directory. There was none. She went down the column of Greenwalds, checking each number. ES was 37 in modern usage. There wasn't a Greenwald with a 37 number.

She dialed it anyway. On the fourth ring, a young female voice answered.

"I'm trying to reach the family of Murray Greenwald," Lee said.

"Who?" In the background, a baby was screeching the way only a newborn could.

"Murray Greenwald?" she said hopefully, although she had lost all hope as soon as the phone had been answered. She repeated the phone number.

"That's the right number, but there's no one here by that name. We've had the number for a year. I really have to go."

"Thank you."

If the Greenwalds had been in their thirties in 1945, they would be in their seventies now. They might be older. They might be in Florida. They might be dead.

She dialed a number for an M. Greenwald. A woman answered, an older woman.

"I'm looking for the family of Murray Greenwald," Lee said. "I'm sorry. You got the wrong Greenwald, dear. This is Morris."

127

"Thank you. Sorry I bothered you."

She tried another. There was no answer. She looked up Mandelbaum. There was a Simon. She dialed. No one answered. She wrote the number down and next to it, "Try again." She called the S. Mandelbaums. One wasn't home. One was a Seymour.

There was a knock on her door. "Come on in."

Lisa came in with a sheet of notepaper. "Your Doctor Singer went to Germany and never came back, at least not to B.U. His last address was Beethoven something."

"Beethovenstrasse."

"Yeah." Lisa smiled. "Something like that. They have no records for him after that."

"Thanks, Lisa." She noticed that she felt relieved. She would not be flying up to Boston tomorrow to see Rich.

"I'm not done," Lisa said with a little smile. "You think I give up that easy?"

"What do you have?"

"Well I had a nice talk with the girl in records, and she gave me the name and phone number of a professor that's been there since nineteen sixty-one. How's that?"

"That's very good." She held out her hand for the piece of paper. "That's really terrific."

"Well, like I figured, someone might remember him. Want me to call?"

"Thanks, I'll do it." She looked at the paper. Carter Hastings. Office hours: Tues. 9-10:30, Thurs. 2-4.

"Anything else you want me to do? That was kind of fun."

"There may be, but not right now. Thanks, Lisa. That was really very good."

She ordered lunch and kept working her way through Simon and S. Mandelbaums. She had completed Brooklyn, Manhattan, and the Bronx, when it suddenly occurred to her that she had given up on the Greenwalds too soon. She refolded her notepaper, got her coat, and left the office.

With the help of a map from a stationery store downstairs, she took the BMT Brighton Beach express train to Kings Highway. From there it was a short walk to East Eighteenth Street, and from there only another block and a half to the address of Murray Greenwald.

The building was prewar, a small six-storey apartment house on a street of privately owned homes and an occasional old red brick apartment house. Mothers pushed baby carriages. Children played on the sidewalk. There was virtually no traffic.

The super's apartment was in the basement, and she took an old, slow elevator down from the ground floor. When she knocked, the super himself opened the door. He was a young, plump black man with a little beard. Out of sight but not far away were sounds of other family members, a woman, children, probably a baby.

"I'm looking for someone who used to live in this building," Lee said, feeling like a very broken record. "Greenwald. Murray Greenwald and his wife."

"Don't know 'em."

"They may have lived here a long time ago. How long have you been here?"

"Three years." It sounded more like a question.

"They might have moved away three or four years ago. Do you know who was the super before you?"

"You don't want him. He only stayed six months. You want the guy before him, Jack Brodie. He retired."

"Do you know where he lives?"

"Hold on." He turned toward the interior of the apart-

129

ment and called, "Vernell?"

A young, rather pretty woman holding a toddler came to the door.

"You know where Jack Brodie went? This lady lookin' for him."

"Take her." She deposited the child in her husband's arms and disappeared.

"She's very pretty," Lee said, looking at the little girl. "She looks kind of tired."

"Yeah, but she don't want to sleep. Too much action, you know?"

His wife returned with an address book. "They got a house on Long Island," she said. "Ronkonkoma. You want the address?"

"Yes, please."

"Here." She handed Lee the book.

Lee copied down the address. Ronkonkoma was a great distance. It would have to wait for another day, but at least it was a start.

She arrived home exhausted. Today had been her first full day on American time and she had been up early and had kept moving since breakfast. She lay down in the bedroom and slept till six, waking with a welcome surge of energy. In the kitchen, she looked around to see what there was that might pass for a light dinner. There were a few carefully labeled packages of home baked leftovers in the freezer, enough that she wouldn't have to shop until tomorrow. She pulled out a chunk of lasagna that she remembered taking home from a friend's party. Before sticking it in the microwave, she listened to the answering machine tape. There had been so many calls when she played it last night, she had done nothing more than make a note of each name. Surely, she hoped, there would be nothing this evening.

There was one call.

"Lee, this is a voice from your mysterious past. It's Sally once-upon-a-time Gordon and I'm spending the weekend in the city. I'd love to see you any breakfast, lunch, or dinner that you're free. I'm staying at the Algonquin because it's so cozily literary, on Forty-something Street. Call and confirm that you're alive. It felt good just listening to your recorded voice. It hasn't changed. Oh, I'm registered as Bollinger."

"Sally, my God." She said it aloud, excited. Sally's voice, too, had sounded just the same. She took the lasagna, tossed it back in the freezer, and looked up the Algonquin.

A sleepy voice answered.

"Sally? This is Lee."

"Lee." It was almost a squeal, rather indelicate for a woman near fifty. "Have you eaten?"

"Not yet."

"Then come right over. We'll have our own round table."

"Give me half an hour."

She took a taxi to the Algonquin. She had seen Sally a few times in the intervening years and they exchanged notes at each year's end. Sally's life had taken a turn for the worse at the end of the year in Germany, around the time that Lee was entering her own crisis. She had wanted to tell Sally what was happening and ask for advice. There was no one else to talk to — Marlies was too young, Frau Biehl was a different generation — and she had to talk to someone. She knew she could count on Sally's sympathy as well as on

131

her quick wisdom. But quite suddenly, Sally stopped show-ing up for lunch at the Mensa.

Finally, Lee called the Gordon apartment. A curt, tight-lipped Sally answered and said yes, she would be at lunch tomorrow. Good-bye.

They decided to forego the usual swill and went to the cafe for a light, quiet, expensive lunch. Sally looked awful. Her face had withered. Lee had sought her out for support but seeing her, she offered it instead.

"What's wrong, Sally?" she said, as they sat at a table overlooking the lower city.

"I'm staying on for another year."

"You told me. You said you could finish the project."

"Sam is taking Wendy and going home."

"What?"

"I can't work if she stays and Sam won't put in another year."

"But that's — that's like a separation."

"Isn't it."

"And if you go back with him?"

"The year is lost and I'm nowhere. I can't get a job with-out a Ph.D. Someone in this goddam family has to earn a living."

"I'm so sorry."

Sally looked across the little table with moist eyes. She put a hand over Lee's. "Thanks, sweetie," she said. "I think I wanted to hear those words more than any other in the En-glish language."

Sally was waiting in the lobby. They hugged and kissed and got a table for dinner.

"You look wonderful, Sally."

132

"I color my hair."

"So do half the women in the country over fifteen. How's my little Wendy?"

"Little Wendy is twenty-four and living with an artist — a sculptor — down in the Village. She writes, she paints, she sings, she's just wonderful. And she's very gorgeous. She looks like me."

Lee laughed. "It's so good to be with you, Sally. I've just come back from Germany."

"Not from our old haunt?"

"Yes."

"I've never been back."

"I've visited the Biehls frequently. This time there was a death in the family."

"Oh?"

"Their youngest daughter."

"Not that little twelve-year-old?" Sally looked horrified.

"No. They had one the year after I left. She just died. She was nineteen."

"How good of you to go."

"They were very special. To me."

"It's a long time, isn't it?"

"Yes. How's your husband?"

"Art? We're divorced. How many years is it since I've seen you? I'm living with a philosopher now. We coauthored a paper a couple of years ago and one thing led to another. What about you?"

"I live alone."

"Just for the time being. No kids from your marriage?"

"No."

"Maybe that's why it didn't work out."

"Partly."

"Did you see a fertility expert?"

"No."

"They can do things, you know."

"It was a bone of contention."

"Ah." Sally looked her old wise self. "Men get touchy about that sort of thing."

"Remember the woman in the village who told me the story of the little boy she kept during the war?"

"Remember! I cried over the tape."

"I never looked for him, Sally."

"You were young and you had other things on your mind."

It was what she liked most about Sally. As cynical as her views often were, she was quick to defend, quick to reassure. "I'm looking for him now."

"Not easy after so many years."

"Let me tell you what I've been doing today."

It was Sally's feeling that Lee should go out to Ronkonkoma to speak to the retired super personally. Let him see she was a nice, nonthreatening lady. It would be too easy over the phone for them to hang up and then they might refuse to speak to her if she came in person.

"I'll do that. I think I'll go tomorrow."

"What ever happened to the guy?" Sally asked and Lee felt her face redden.

"Rich?"

"Rich. Exactly."

"I think he went back to his wife."

"Shit."

"My sentiments exactly."

They ate and talked and Sally pulled out pictures of Wendy and her sculptor. Wendy did indeed look like Sally. She also looked happy.

"Does she see her father much?" Lee asked.

"They've always been on good terms."

"Since that year."

"The year that he played mommy. That was the year." Sally looked thoughtful. She played with her napkin, folding it, unfolding it. "I never really told you the whole story. About Sam and the book and the rest of it."

"The book he was writing? Did he actually get it published?"

"Made a mint," Sally said. "When we divorced, I got half. I felt I'd earned it."

"I looked for his name for years in bookstores."

"He used his middle name. It's fancier. Antonio Gordon. Ring a bell?"

"More like a gong. I think I even read one of his books under a palm tree."

"You and every other literate American over puberty. But there's more."

"More of what?"

"More of Sam besides the book. He remarried the day after our divorce. A German woman. Someone he met in the sandbox while he was minding Wendy."

"I see."

"I couldn't talk about it for years. Sam was the first American house-husband. Did you know that?"

"You did rather foreshadow American family life."

"With all its lurid twists."

"Is he still married to her?"

"Oh, yes. They had two children together, besides her daughter from Germany and Wendy." Sally smiled. "Then, a couple of years ago, she went to law school."

Chapter Two

Lee picked up the latest Antonio Gordon in the Penn Station bookstore and bought a round-trip ticket to Ronkonkoma. The picture on the back of the jacket showed a smiling Sam Gordon with a graying beard and a deeply receding hairline. On the flap, Sam was described as the author of ten novels, married to Berthe, and the father of four children. He and his wife lived in Greenwich in a restored old house with fruit trees and a pond.

During the two-hour trip she was able to read the first four chapters. For all the depth and intellect Sam had displayed during the year in Germany, he wrote pleasantly readable trash. His main female character was a woman who started law school on her fortieth birthday. Lee sighed. She had thought the Gordons' marriage the most solid and rewarding she had ever seen among people in her generation. So much for the astute observations of a twenty-two-year-old.

The Brodies' house turned out to be pleasant walking distance from the station. It was a two-storey wooden house on a street of similar old houses, some of them not very well cared for. The Brodies' house had the best lawn on the street with shrubs showing signs of renewed life.

She walked up the four steps to the front porch and rang the bell.

A pleasant-looking older woman opened the door. "Yes?"

"Mrs. Brodie?"

"That's right."

"I'm Lee Linden and I'm looking for a family that lived in your house in Brooklyn."

"Eighteenth Street?" she said, perking up.

"Yes. Their name was Greenwald."

"Five-D," Mrs. Brodie said. "Come on in." She turned toward the interior of the house and called, "Jack? Can you come down for a minute?" She turned back to Lee. "He'll be right down. He has to rest now. Heart."

"I hope I'm not disturbing you."

"Oh, no. We don't get much company. Sit down."

She sat in an easy chair that had so many pillows on it, it was hard to be comfortable. Mrs. Brodie came over and removed some of them with embarrassment, mumbling an apology. She tossed them on the sofa which already had its share. Then she sat down as a tall, lean, stooped man with sparse graying hair came into the living room.

"This is my husband, Jack. Jack, this is Mrs. —"

"Linden." She stood and shook hands.

"Nice to make your acquaintance."

"Mrs. Linden wants to know about the Greenwalds."

"Five-D. Sure, nice folks. Quiet. Never asked for

137

much." He sat on the sofa, pushing pillows out of the way. "Had a problem in their bathroom. Water stains on the wall behind the tub. Went on for years. Never found out what caused it. Prob'ly Six-D, but they swore it weren't their fault. Green, they kept that bathroom. Every time we painted, had to be green."

"I'm looking for one of their children," Lee said.

"Three kids," the super recited. "Two boys and a girl. Nice, quiet kids. Never gave us no trouble."

"Simon is the one I'm looking for."

Jack Brodie pouted his lips and shook his head. "No Simon."

"You're sure?"

"Positive."

"When did you start to work in that building?"

He turned to his wife. "When was it, Millie? Forty-eight?"

"Forty-eight," she confirmed. "October. We left in eighty-two. Thirty-four years. Don't seem it, does it, Jack?"

"Nope."

"Do you remember the children's names?" Lee asked.

"The girl was—" he looked at his wife— "Barbara. The boys were Joe, I remember, and Steve."

"Steve," Lee repeated. "Do you remember how old Steve was when you moved in?"

"Ten maybe. Hard to recall. Eight. Little fellow, dark hair. They all grew. Hard to remember back that far."

"And Mr. and Mrs. Greenwald," Lee said. "What happened to them?"

"He died," Mrs. Brodie said. "I remember the night.

138

All the crying. Police came. Ambulance. He was dead when they carried him out."

"And Mrs. Greenwald?"

"Florida," the Brodies said in unison.

"You wouldn't recall where in Florida, would you?" They looked at each other. Then Jack Brodie smiled. "Don't everyone go to Miami Beach?"

"I guess they do," Lee said. "About how long ago did she move?"

"Seventies. Ten years?" He looked at his wife.

"Maybe eight," she said.

"Do you know what happened to the children?"

"She married," Mr. Brodie said. "Couldn't tell you the name. The boys—they moved out."

"Joey always came back," Mrs. Brodie said. "He visited a lot. On Saturday, usually. He musta lived nearby."

"You wouldn't happen to know what Mrs. Greenwald's first name was, would you?"

"Esther," Jack Brodie said quickly. "Esther Greenwald."

"Thank you very much." Lee stood. "I wonder if you could tell me—ES in the telephone number. What did that stand for?"

Mrs. Brodie beamed. "Esplanade. We all had Esplanade six numbers in those days. Could I get you a cup of coffee?"

"No, thank you. Thank you very much for your help."

"What's it for?" the super asked. "They come into money?"

"No. Someone from a long time ago is looking for— one of the Greenwald boys."

"I hope you find 'em."

"They was nice people," Mrs. Brodie said. "Nice family. I remember the night he died. What an awful night that was."

"Never figured out what caused that water stain," Jack Brodie said. "In that green bathroom."

She read four more chapters of Antonio Gordon on the way back to New York and knew as she closed the book in Penn Station that she would never finish it.

At home she checked the Manhattan telephone book. There were Joseph Greenwalds and J. Greenwalds. She called them all without success. Then she sat down in one of her own comfortable chairs and closed her eyes.

Looking for Simon Mandelbaum was a tonic. It kept her from thinking of Rich. She almost wished she had confided in Sally. It would be good to talk to someone, to hear what someone else had to say. When she found him, if she found him, she wondered whether she would have the courage to talk to him, whether dredging up a brief affair of two decades past was foolhardy.

But it hadn't been just a brief affair. It had changed her life. And she needed to know, while memory still served them both, whether it had changed his. Moving on in life had become connected with tying up what had happened in Germany. Twenty years ago.

She got up and found a record, the Waldstein. Beethoven. Beethovenstrasse. Beethovenplatz. She put it on the turntable and sat down again to listen. There had been no music in their relationship. Neither of them had had a record player or records. There had been times when they were together when it would have been nice to hear music, music like this. She closed her eyes again, anticipating the beautiful, lyrical theme. It would take awhile. Beethoven made you wait for it. But like all good things, when it happened, it was wonderful.

On Sunday she went quickly through the *Times*, dressed, and went down to the studio. She liked it when it was empty. The quiet was soothing. The sound studios were dark and empty, the control rooms at rest.

She went to Lisa's cabinet and pulled out the directories for the four other boroughs besides Manhattan. If Joseph Greenwald wasn't in the city, how would she ever find him? He could be anywhere in the country. And how many Esther Greenwalds might there be in the state of Florida?

She tried Brooklyn with no luck and one no answer. Where do people go when they leave Brooklyn? Long Island, of course, but that task was monumental. Long Island was a thousand little towns and who knew how many phone books. She tried Queens.

The first two were negatives. On the third one, a woman answered.

"I'm looking for the Joseph Greenwald who is the son of Murray and Esther Greenwald," Lee said, trying not to sound like a broken record.

"Just a minute." The woman called, "Joe?" in a voice that receded in the distance. "Telephone. I think something's wrong with your mother."

141

A man came on suddenly and said, "Hello. What's wrong?" in a tense voice.

"Mr. Greenwald, I'm trying—"

"What's wrong with my mother?"

"Mr. Greenwald, I asked your wife if you were the son of Murray and Esther Greenwald. I think she misinterpreted my question."

"Oh. Thank God. Sorry. What can I do for you?"

"I'm looking for Simon Mandelbaum."

She heard him let his breath out. Then he said, "You know, there is no Simon Mandelbaum."

"What do you mean? Has something happened to him?"

"Who is this?"

"My name is Lee Linden. Twenty years ago I was a student in Germany. While I was there, I met a woman who protected a young boy during the war. His name was Simon Mandelbaum."

"Jesus Christ."

She waited but nothing happened. "Mr. Greenwald?"

"Are you in the city, miss?"

"Yes."

"Could I see you, maybe tomorrow? We could have lunch. There's a nice deli near where I work."

"Lunch would be fine."

"OK." He gave her an address in lower Manhattan. "Make it before twelve. It gets pretty crowded."

"I'll be there. Mr. Greenwald, is Simon alive?"

"Yeah. He's alive."

"Thank God," she said, and hung up.

She felt jittery with excitement. A nearly hopeless task had suddenly come close to being accomplished.

142

She took the four directories and went to Lisa's work area. As she was putting them back in the cabinet, she heard a door close.

"Someone here?" she called.

"I thought you were taking time off."

"Cal. Hi. I am. I needed phone books. I've just taken a giant step forward. I'm feeling pretty good." She closed the cabinet and stood.

"Come into my office." He touched her shoulder and guided her. In the office, he took off his coat and tossed it over a chair. "Sit down. We can share the coffee and sandwich." He was carrying a familiar bag from the takeout down the block.

"I'm not hungry. Thanks."

They sat at the table that was used for conferences, parties, lunches, and nearly every other activity that couldn't be handled at a desk or in the sound studio.

"I am worried about you," he said, leaving the bag unopened.

"There's nothing to worry about, Cal."

"I don't like it when people say they have to put their lives together."

"Eat your lunch."

He opened the bag and took out a large container of coffee and a sandwich. "Want to talk about it?"

Some of it, she thought. Talk to someone who cares about her. Talk about it in English. See how it plays in translation. "I was a student in Germany," she said, "twenty, twenty-one years ago. I met an American there. He was teaching at the University of Frankfurt. We fell in love."

"And I thought you were pure as driven snow when I met you."

143

"No you didn't."

"Sorry. Go on."

"He was separated from his wife. She was in the States. I was going to stay on for a second year and live with him in Frankfurt. At just about the time that I had to make all the arrangements, his wife showed up. I waited as long as I was able and left. I never saw him again."

"Just like that? Wasn't that rather precipitous?"

"I had travel arrangements to make. I was a kid, a *student*. My funds were down to nothing. I had no resources. You could measure my savings in single dollars, not thousands. I couldn't hang around waiting. Every day cost me. I made a decision."

"Maybe she came to talk to him about a divorce," Cal said in his calm, patient voice. "Maybe it was ending."

"Maybe it was." She looked at the steam rising from his coffee. "It wasn't, Cal. She showed up at his apartment with her suitcase and she moved in. She didn't go to a hotel, she stayed with him. I couldn't bear to think—" She stood and walked away from the table, to the other end of his office where he had pictures on the wall and bookcases. "He didn't belong to her anymore, he belonged to me. She had no right to impose herself on him, and he shouldn't have let her stay." She could feel her throat tightening, her eyes filling.

"It's not easy to throw someone out." His voice was so calm, so soothing. "Especially someone like that. You get her angry, there's no telling what she'll do, hold up the divorce, attach your property and savings. The fact that she stayed with him doesn't mean they slept together."

144

"I loved him." It came out in a whisper. She went to his desk and opened the drawer where she knew he kept a box of Kleenex. "How can I care so much after so long?" She sat in his chair, crying quietly.

"Because it was important. Why did you marry Ted?"

"I thought I loved him."

"He was never the right person for you."

"I don't know that. I know I wasn't the right person for him. I owe him an apology. Maybe, when this is over, I'll give it to him. If he'll let me."

"When what's over?"

She blotted her face and tossed the tissue. "I'm going to find him." She said it resolutely. For the first time since she had been in Germany for the funeral, she felt she meant it. She would find Rich. She would see him. They would talk.

"What for? After all this time."

"I want to see him. Look at him. Let him see me. I don't look bad, do I?"

"You look fine. Great."

"I guess I'd like to know if he ever left her. What I really want to know is if it was real."

"And if it wasn't?"

"Then maybe I can get on with my life."

"You haven't done so badly."

"I can do better. I want to do better."

"I think you'll find it was real."

She looked at him. He had pushed himself away from the table, stuffed the papers in the bag, rested an ankle on a knee. "Why do you say that?"

"Because I know you. Because you wouldn't have given your heart away—and your virginity, I take it,

145

at a time when that wasn't done casually—to someone who would two-time his wife and then two-time you. Did he tell you he was married?"

"Yes."

"So there you are. An honorable man put in a situation from which there wasn't any easy extrication. If you'd waited awhile, it would probably have all worked out."

"You're a very nice person, Cal," she said. "I think I don't tell you that often enough. You're everything a friend should be."

"Is that why it never worked out with us? Because of what happened then?"

She shook her head. "I told you. You and I are business partners. There's no room for that kind of feeling in our relationship. And besides, I like your wife. I really like your wife."

She got down to the delicatessen at a quarter to twelve. It was still three-quarters empty and the harried man who seemed to run everything said, Yeah, he knew Joey Greenwald and sit over there, I'll send him to your table when he comes in. She ordered a Coke with a piece of lemon and looked over the menu. It had more content than eight chapters of Sam Gordon's latest novel. It would have taken half the trip to Ronkonkoma to read every entry.

"Miss Linden?"

She looked up. "Yes. Mr. Greenwald?"

"Joe." He held out his hand. "Nice to meet you." They shook hands and he sat. "You order yet?"

"No."

He waved a hand and a white-aproned waiter appeared. She ordered roast beef on rye and Joe Greenwald ordered a sandwich by number and a glass of beer.

"So," he said. He was about her age, perhaps a few years older, graying and slightly overweight, not a bad-looking man.

"Thank you very much for seeing me."

"How'd you find me?"

"The phone book. The Brodies told me your name."

"The Brodies. My God, how are the Brodies? They were so good to my mother after Pop died."

"They seem to be fine. They had only good things to say about your family."

"Well, I was nice to them, too, if you understand what I mean."

"Yes."

"And you just looked up all the Joe Greenwalds till you found me."

"That's right."

"Let me get this straight. You met a woman in Germany who said she knew Simon Mandelbaum when he was a boy."

"I met a woman who kept him in her home during the war, Mr. Greenwald."

"Joey."

Lee smiled. "She protected him. She kept him from being arrested which, as I'm sure you know, meant death."

"Right. And when did you meet her?"

"Twenty years ago."

"So how come it's taken twenty years for you to look for Simon Mandelbaum?"

How come indeed. Because I fell in love with Richard Singer, Joe Greenwald, and nothing in my life happened easily after that. "Certain things happened," she said carefully, "that prevented me from looking for him. I was recently back in Germany and I remembered my promise to the woman."

"What promise?"

"To find him and tell him that she loves him like a son."

"I see."

The waiter came with the sandwiches. The one in front of Joe Greenwald looked almost too large for a mortal mouth.

"Nice, Harry," he said. "Looks good." He took a bite as though he had practiced, chewed, swallowed, drank some beer. "You know what my cousin went through with those people?"

"I have some idea."

"They stuck him down in a cellar. It wasn't any basement apartment, believe me. It was a *cellar*. You know what you live with in a cellar?"

"Joey," she said, "do you know what was out on the street? The SS was out on the street. Neighbors who would betray him were out on the street. When it was dangerous, she put him in the cellar. There were nights she slept down there with him."

"You know—what's your first name?"

"Lee."

"Lee. Can I call you Lee?"

"Yes."

"You know, Lee, I was only a little kid when they brought him home, but that was just a two-bedroom apartment we had in Brooklyn. It's not like today, every kid has his own room. The three of us shared a bedroom, my sister, my cousin, and me. I remember the nightmares. He used to wake up in the middle of the night. My mother had to come and take care of him, night after night. That kid lived through hell."

"Is that why he changed his name?"

Joey put his beer glass down and leaned back. "I come from a paranoid family, you know what I mean? They never made waves. Things went wrong, they lived with them. Don't make a fuss, no one'll remember you. A hundred things went wrong in that apartment, they never called Jack Brodie, except for one thing, one damned thing and he never fixed it. They wanted to be anonymous.

"My parents got out of Germany by the skin of their teeth. Most of the family didn't make it. The Mandelbaums didn't. A lot of others didn't. When my parents heard there was one goddam little kid who had made it through the war, they couldn't wait to get him and bring him home. It was like he was the only one left in a whole lost tribe and my parents didn't want to see the tribe die. They nourished him. You know, be fruitful and multiply. They did what they could."

"How did they know where to find him?"

"I guess his father wrote a letter before they took him away. Don't ask me how he got it out. A neighbor maybe. I don't know. The letter went to my grandmother. I heard this story a hundred times when I was growing up. They took a chance when they went over. Thank God it paid off. That was no easy place to find or to get to."

"I know."

"Anyway, they got him back, they took care of him,

149

but they were never happy people, you know what I mean? My father was a man who looked over his shoulder. It was an evil world. It was full of Hitlers waiting to kill babies. They changed their name from Grunwald to Greenwald when they came over and the next thing they wanted to do was change it again to Greenwood, but I stopped them. When my cousin was eighteen, he went into court and became Steven Greene. With an *e* at the end. They'd been calling him Steve for years. It's a nice clean American name. Hitler'll never find him. And his phone is unlisted. So don't even try."

"I hope you'll tell me how to reach him."

"I don't know if I will. He's not a stable guy, my cousin. He has my father's paranoia and he has his own memories. It's not such a great combination."

"Does he have children?"

"Oh yeah, he has kids."

"I think what I have for him will make him a happier person."

"What do you mean, what you have for him?"

"I have a tape recording."

"From the woman in Germany?"

"Yes."

"What does she say?"

"How he came to her. A little about his mother and father."

"His mother and father? She knew them?"

"Yes."

He wiped his mouth on the napkin and poured the remainder of his beer. "I'm g'na call my cousin and get back to you. If he wants to see you, we'll drive up together, maybe next weekend. He doesn't live in the city."

"That's fine with me."

"You have this tape with you?"

"No."

"But you'll give it to him."

"It's an old reel-to-reel. I'll make a cassette for him."

"That's fine. He's got all the equipment to play that stuff."

"Here's my number." She took a business card out of her bag and wrote her home phone number on it. "Thank you, Joey."

"Not yet," he said. "We'll see how it goes."

Chapter Three

He didn't call her that night and she wondered, sitting in her apartment after returning half the calls that had come in while she was in Germany, whether Joey had called him, whether Simon Mandelbaum, a.k.a. Steven Greene, was torturing himself over his cousin's proposition. She had imagined finding him, walking up to his door, giving a brief explanation, handing him the tape, and watching him rejoice in happy and grateful memories of the Möcks. With Joey Greenwald as an intermediary, it had gotten out of hand. It had become an event. If Joey talked to his cousin in a certain way, she would never get to see him. If he talked to his cousin at all . . .

She slept badly Monday night. Tuesday morning Professor Carter Hastings had office hours from nine to ten-thirty and she intended to call him. She awoke early, dressed, breakfasted, and waited. At nine-fifteen she would pick up the phone and dial Boston. She watched the kitchen clock, feeling the sense of anticipation grow with every slow minute.

At eleven minutes after, the phone rang. It was Joey Greenwald.

"Suppose I listen to the tape first," he said. "Then make up my mind about my cousin."

He had not called his cousin after all. She felt angry enough to explode. She had had enough of paranoia, of protecting people old enough to protect themselves, of manipulating people's lives, of living with water stains in green bathrooms.

"I want to give the tape to Steven Greene," she said. "The tape is not meant for anyone else. If you won't call your cousin, I'm prepared to hire a private detective to find him."

"OK, OK. I just thought . . . Let me call him right away and I'll get back to you."

"Thank you." She hung up, feeling much better. It was still not nine-fifteen. She decided to give it ten more minutes.

Joey Greenwald called back in less time than that. "Can you go on Saturday?" he asked.

"Yes."

"I'll pick you up at ten."

"Where are we going?"

"Upstate. It's near White Plains."

"I'll be in front of my building at ten."

She hung up with relief. The tough part was just coming up.

Professor Carter Hastings answered on the first ring. He had a thin, wiry voice but it was friendly.

"Good morning," Lee said when he had identified himself. "Professor Hastings, I'm trying to locate someone who was in your department in the sixties. His name is Richard Singer."

"Richard, yes. He hasn't been with us for a while."

"The secretary thought you might know where he is now."

"Well, let's see. My, I haven't thought of Richard for a while. He left to teach in Germany and my recollection is he never came back, at least not to B.U. We got Christmas cards from him for a while."

"Do you recall from where?"

"Not offhand, but my wife would know. Are you a former student of his?"

"Yes, I am."

"Well I'm sure he'd like to see you. Why don't you give me your number and I'll call you back after I've talked to my wife."

"Perhaps I can call you. I'm in New York."

"New York." He sounded surprised. "I thought you were right here on campus. Why don't you call back about three this afternoon?"

"Thank you, I will."

"What was your name?"

"Lee Linden."

"Fine, Ms. Linden. Three o'clock."

She wasn't sure what to expect but she felt good about Simon Mandelbaum. She dug up the old tape, took it in to the office and played it. The sound was fine, Frau Möck's voice loud and clear. She made two copies on standard cassettes, labeled them, and dropped them in her bag.

Cal came by, saw her, asked her if she would mind looking over a contract. She welcomed it. It was nice money for three sound tapes and a video to be shot on

154

location in the offices of the contracting company, part of a nationwide training course with guaranteed repeat orders. It felt good to use her brain on something clean and cold. She made notes on Post-Its and stuck them on the appropriate pages. Later, Cal thanked her for picking up something he had overlooked.

At ten after three, she called Boston.

"Ms. Linden, yes, hello," the professor said. "My wife dug up her Christmas lists. She says we haven't heard from them for about ten years."

She heard "them" and flinched. "Do you know where he was ten years ago?"

"Well, it seems he bounced around for awhile after Germany. She remembers there were a lot of addresses that she discarded, but she does have the last one. I'm afraid he isn't there anymore. She sent a Christmas card there one year and it was returned. It was Washington, D.C. I think he may have left teaching."

"Washington," she repeated.

He dictated the address and she wrote it down. "I'm not sure there's much more I can do for you."

"You wouldn't know anyone who was a friend of his in those days."

"It's so long ago," the voice on the phone said. "I wish I could . . . Well, maybe there is something else I can do."

She held her breath.

"A lot of these fellows keep their memberships in the professional societies, even after they give up teaching. Makes 'em feel they still have a hand in it. I'll have a look at the membership lists. Want to call me tomorrow at about," he paused, "oh, three-thirty? My last class ends at three."

"I'll be glad to. Thank you very much for your trouble."

"Oh, no trouble. Happy to help out."

She floated through the next twenty-four hours, her eye on the nearest clock or on her watch. A surge of optimism propelled her. She would find him. She had a location and an indication that he was in business or government. That might keep him in one place. She called Washington information and asked for Richard Singer but there was none.

In the office there were the makings of a disaster. They had been scheduled to shoot a commercial at ten in the morning using a model in a red barrel. The barrel was painted at seven in the morning and refused to dry. The actress who was to peer out of it wearing a white bathing suit sat for hours looking disgusted. Every five minutes someone would touch the inside of the barrel and come away with a red fingertip. By afternoon everyone in the place had a handful of red fingertips.

Cal was fit to be tied. "They promised me quick-drying paint," he complained when Lee met him in a hall. "It's almost eight hours."

"In a lifetime that's not very much."

"Only someone who would wait twenty years to look for an old boyfriend could say something that cruel."

She laughed. "Have they tried blowing on it?"

"Hairdryers. Fans. I can't believe this is happening."

"See you later, Cal," she called cheerfully, walking off to her office.

At twenty to four she called Boston. The professor answered again on the first ring.

"I may have something for you," he said, sounding

156

quite as cheerful as she had a few minutes earlier. "He's not in the most recent directories but about five years ago he was listed as a member of the Historical Association. Got a pencil?"

"Yes." Her voice nearly paralyzed.

"Black and Singer Associates," he read off. "Probably some kind of consulting firm. Washington's full of them." He gave her the address and she thanked him. Then she thanked him again. Then she hung up.

When she had her voice under control, she called Washington information. Black and Singer Associates was listed at the same address Professor Hastings had given her. She hung up, shaking. She had found him.

She went down to the lobby before ten on Saturday morning and asked the doorman to look out for Joey Greenwald. It was overcast and damp but not raining. In her bag was the cassette for Steven Greene. She had played it on a very ordinary tape recorder and was pleased with the quality. She wondered if he remembered German. She wondered a lot of things.

About five after ten the doorman signaled her and she went outside. Joey Greenwald stood beside a black Buick. She called good morning and slid inside. He drove over to the FDR, picked up the Deegan, and drove north.

He talked the entire way, exhausting her. He talked about his wife, his sons, his daughter, his house in Queens, his mother's retirement home, the weather in Florida, and so many other things that she lost track of them. He asked very few questions, for which she was grateful. She did not wish to share any part of her life with him although she did not dislike him.

When he finally turned off the highway, he made his way through a beautiful suburb with daffodils in bloom and lawns greening up.

"This is it," he said, and turned into a driveway beside a large brick ranch with many large, carefully tended shrubs. He stopped the car at the top of the driveway and opened his door. "Come on. I'll take you in the front way; you're a guest."

The door was opened immediately by a pretty woman about Lee's age or a little older. She smiled, shook hands, took coats, and led them into the living room, a large, carpeted room overlooking a huge piece of lush property at the rear of the house. A thin, dark-haired, graying man rose from a big comfortable chair as they entered the room.

"Lee," Joey said, "my cousin Steve. Steve, Lee Linden."

They shook hands. "I'm so glad to have found you," Lee began, feeling the wonder of the moment, the magic of having put together a tale of heroism with a real human being. "I was a student in Germany twenty years ago—"

"Please sit down," Harriet Greene said. "Can I bring you something to eat?"

"No, thank you," Lee said, sitting on the sofa facing the picture window.

"You're sure? A cold drink?"

"Go on," Steven Greene said.

"I lived in a city north of Frankfurt, south of Kassel. My research took me to a little village. For a number of months, I visited a woman named Frau Möck."

"Möck," he repeated, his face changing.

"That's right."

"Are you all right, Steve?" his wife asked, her voice tinged with concern.

"Harriet," Steven Greene said, "you and Joey, would you go to the family room and catch up together? I'd like to talk to this lady alone."

Joey and Harriet looked at Steve, then got up and left the room.

"I'm sorry," Steven Greene said, "you were saying."

"She didn't know I was Jewish until the very end, the end of this tape." She took it out of her bag and handed it to him. He inspected it as if its contents were spread over its surface. "After many sessions in which we talked about the war, when we were just about finished, she told me this story. I intended to find you twenty years ago—I should have—but I wasn't able to. I apologize for that."

"Möck," he said again, shaping his lips around the alien sound, enunciating it perfectly.

"You remember the name."

"I remember." He was very pale. "You were in that house."

"Many times. We sat in the kitchen."

"That house," he said softly, his eyes unfocused.

His face was so pale she wished his wife had stayed, to rescue him if he became ill.

"Mr. Greene," she said, "I didn't want to make this a social occasion. Your cousin Joe insisted on driving me up here. All I wanted was to give you the tape and leave you. There are things I could say to you but really, everything is on the tape. I couldn't say it more eloquently." She took a business card from her bag, wrote her home phone number on it, and handed it to him. "If you want to talk to me afterward, if you want to hear any of my other tapes, give me a call." She stood.

"Thank you." He rose from his chair.

She stood there feeling awkward. If she had done this twenty years ago, much of her youthful excitement would have communicated itself. But it wasn't then, it was now, and the difference between the girl she had been and the woman she had become was evident in her awkward silence. She had never been sure how this meeting would turn out but she could not have imagined it quite like this. She wanted to say something wonderful, an introduction and conclusion to the tape, something he would remember as he listened, think of afterward. Something short.

"She really cares for you," she said finally, her voice catching.

His dark eyes widened momentarily and Lee turned and walked out of the living room.

The drive home seemed shorter. It had been difficult to get Joe Greenwald to leave so soon after arriving, and with nothing to eat, but she had accomplished her mission and she hadn't asked for the ride anyway.

"What does he do?" she asked when they were on the highway.

"Accountant. It's a good job for him. He can work with numbers, doesn't have to mess around with people."

"My accountant messes around with people."

"Yeah? Well, you know what I mean."

"Why don't you drop me at a subway near where you live? I can get home by myself."

"Don't be silly."

He left her at her apartment about one-thirty. The whole adventure had taken little more than three hours, nearly two thirds of that driving. She thanked him and said good-bye.

Then she went upstairs and made a reservation at a hotel in Washington for the next night. The time had come.

Chapter Four

She checked into the Mayflower on Sunday afternoon and looked over a map of Washington she had carried with her. The address of Black and Singer Associates was walkable and she decided to walk it. She took her time, taking in the sights, turning for the many picturesque views Washington offered with its streets radiating from a center and its monuments placed strategically for best effect.

She had planned nothing, not the time she would arrive tomorrow, not what she would say when she finally faced him. All she was sure of was the increasing tension as she neared the address, the location on the map, the building that Rich had his office in. There was something mathematically clever about that; tension increases in inverse proportion to distance. By the time she turned the last corner, she could scarcely swallow. Damn! Today she was only scouting out the location, finding her way. There was a whole twenty-four hours before she could attempt to see him, a whole night to try to sleep through, memories to push away or deal with, finally. Deal with them finally. Speak the truth, out loud, for the first time. Ever.

. She remembered her conversation with Cal just a week ago today, how she had said, out loud: *He didn't belong to her any more; he belonged to me.*

And you let him go.

There wasn't any other way.

She realized she had stopped walking. In front of her was the double door of the building. It was small as office buildings go and not very new looking, but there was something solid in its age, something majestic. She tried the door but it was locked, and she stepped back. It had taken twenty minutes to walk here slowly from the hotel. At a more normal pace, it could be done in fifteen or sixteen. So be it.

"Going in?"

A young woman stood holding the door open.

"Yes, thank you." She smiled and took the door.

"The elevator's not working."

"That's OK."

The woman walked off and Lee let the door close behind her. There was a small directory in the lobby. Black and Singer occupied a suite on the fifth floor. She began to move toward the staircase, aware that she was not thinking, just moving, just allowing a tide that had been held back for half her life to sweep her forward.

The stairs were marble, the bannister cool under her touch. The fifth floor. She remembered saying Greenwald to Mrs. Brodie and hearing her say 5-D. Everything had a five in it. She looked at her watch.

It was nearing five o'clock.

The fifth floor was unlighted except with natural light from a couple of windows at each end. The door to Suite 501 was dark stained oak with a brass nameplate. She walked over to it and turned the handle. It was locked and she felt mightily relieved, as though she had been given a last-minute reprieve from the hangman. She backed away and turned toward the stairs when she heard a voice. Voices.

"OK," the nearer one called from inside the locked door. "I'll be in at eight and take care of it."

The other voice was farther away and she could not make out the response.

"Collins," the nearer voice called. Very near this time, just the other side of the oak door.

A lock turned and the door opened, flooding the hallway with light.

"Looking for someone, ma'am?" He was an older man, sixty or more, dressed casually and carrying an attaché case. His hair and mustache were gray.

"Richard Singer," she said, her voice carrying her through this last, terrible moment.

"You have an appointment?"

"No."

He pulled the door open and started to enter the office.

"No," she said. "Don't. I'll come back tomorrow."

He looked at her, making an assessment. "Why don't you go on in now? He's just finishing up. I'm sure he'll be glad to see you."

"Thank you." She wasn't sure why she said it. She didn't want to go in; she didn't want to see Rich today. She wanted to run, far away, back to Germany,

164

to the arms of Frau Biehl, where she felt safe. Her voice was nearly gone, her throat so tight she might not be able to make herself heard.

She stepped inside. The door closed behind her and she heard a key turn. She was in a reception area with an empty desk and chair. The floor was carpeted, carpeted as far as she could see. Lights were on in this area but beyond it they were off. She walked tentatively, as though each step might set off a land mine.

Beyond the reception area there was a choice of left or right. To the left there was an open door and light. And a voice.

"When does the committee convene?" the voice said.

Funny how voices change so little, how they maintain their essential identity. They age, they lower, but they retain their distinctive quality, that sound that we recognize even over the telephone when most of the overtones have been filtered out. It was a voice she would have known anywhere. It was Rich's.

She leaned against the wall beside the open door, resting, listening to the one-sided conversation.

"You'll have it by noon," she heard him say, her Rich. The telephone was hung up. There were a few other small sounds, papers, the slight squeak of a desk chair swiveling.

She walked silently to the open door feeling none of the exuberance of the twenty-two-year-old who had pulled to the side of the road and called in her best German, "May I help you?" She saw now that that had been another lifetime, a time forever lost. Today she felt panic, a rising hysteria.

Inside, there was a desk to the right, half a wall of books, comfortable chairs and a low table to the left, windows straight ahead.

She knocked twice on the door frame and took one step into the office. He looked up from his desk. He was tieless and in his shirtsleeves. She watched the degrees of recognition pass across his face.

"Hello, Rich," she said, hearing her voice shake.

He said, "Lee."

"Yes."

"Stein."

She nodded.

"You're a little late."

"I know."

He pushed his chair back and stood, circling the desk to his right so that he was farther from her. He shook his head as though casting away shadows. "What did I do wrong?" he said.

The question brought her almost to tears. "Nothing," she said.

"Why don't we sit down."

She unbuttoned her raincoat and let him take it from her, standing and watching as he hung it in a closet next to the door. She sat with her back to the wall of books as he returned and took the chair across the coffee table from her.

"I'm afraid you've destroyed my equanimity," he said.

It made her smile. "Mine's been gone a long time, just thinking about this."

"How did you find me?"

"Carter Hastings."

"Carter. I haven't been in touch with him for ten

or twelve years."

It was a marvel, hearing that voice. His eyes were the same, his hair barely touched with gray at the temples. He had aged beautifully. Even today she would stop at the side of the road and offer this man help.

"He looked you up in an old Historical Association directory. I told him I was a former student."

"You were less easy to find."

"I know that."

"And eventually I decided you didn't want to be."

"It seemed better. At the time."

"Not to me."

"Did you stay on that year?"

"Just for a semester."

"I was in Germany a couple of weeks ago. Frau Biehl asked to be remembered to you. And the girls."

He shook his head. "They were a stone wall when I was looking for you. I must have called a hundred times. Went up there finally. The doctor wouldn't let me past the doorstep. Said you'd gone back to the States and he didn't have your address. Which I didn't have either."

"I want to tell you about it, Rich."

"Does it matter anymore?"

"It does to me. I think it will to you, too."

"That was a very painful part of my life, Lee. I think I got over it by getting angry. Very angry."

"I never did get over it."

He smiled, looked away, and shook his head. "Why don't we let it be? It was a long time ago. I was young, you were young. Even wars don't stay with people forever. Why should a little misunderstanding

167

in Germany?"

"It's not that simple."

The phone on his desk started to ring, startling her. He glanced over at it, then away.

"It'll stop," he said.

She waited and it did. "Did you split up with your wife?" she asked.

"Eventually. After I got back to the States. Is that what it was all about?"

"No."

"Did you marry?"

"After a while. It wasn't a very successful marriage. We've been divorced for a long time now. Years."

"I have a sixteen-year-old son. He lives with his mother."

"That's nice. That you have a son."

"Very nice."

"If you have the time—it won't take very long—I'd just like to tell you—what happened. I'll go away after that. I didn't come down here to rearrange your life. I owe you this. But it's more than that. I think we loved each other once."

"I know we did." His voice was low.

"If tonight isn't good for you—"

"Tonight is fine." He didn't check his watch, which glittered occasionally from the light at the window as he moved. He didn't check his appointment book or call to cancel an engagement. He watched her with an intense interest. Then he reached across the table and touched her cheek with his fingertips.

She wanted to catch his hand and hold it, press it against her, but it was too late—or too soon—for that. Still, the touch washed away a certain fear. Like medicine, it made her breathe more easily. It allowed her to swallow.

"I gave birth to your child in Germany," she said. "A little girl. Her name was Tina."

Chapter Five

It was a season of sweet scents and sweet moments. The drive to Frankfurt became as familiar as the walk to the Mensa. They preferred Frankfurt because Lee could stay overnight without making excuses. The weekends lengthened. She drove down on Friday and came back on Monday. Often she would meet him at the university and they would walk back to Beethovenstrasse together, kissing at streetcorners, touching somewhere between shoulder and hip as they walked, climbing that last, awful flight of steps up the side of his house with an exhilarating final burst of speed. Inside they were together. Inside, before anything else happened, they would make love.

He kissed her again and lay on his back, one knee up. "Hi," he said. He was still out of breath.

"Hi."

"How was your week?"

"A little sad. I drove out to the village for the last time and told Frau Möck the embassy wouldn't help me. She said she never expected them to."

"You'll find him. Tell me about the great love affair, Marlies and what's-his-name."

"Robert Becker."

"Your blood brother. Do they or don't they? Did they or didn't they?"

"I don't know. Marlies acts as if that night never happened."

"She's an honorable woman. Accepts responsibility. I like that kind."

"I think I blushed when I returned the sheets to Sally."

He touched her cheek. "Just a little natural color. Nice color. You are so pretty."

"I am so happy."

And on into June, weekend after weekend, waiting all week for the moment she could get in the car and make the trip, stand at the door to the building where he taught, watch for his familiar figure, the slightly loping walk, the very American summer jacket that he took off the minute he got outside, saw her, kissed her, and started back to Beethovenstrasse with her, talking all the way, catching up on the intervening days, answering questions before they were asked and forgetting to ask the questions that needed to be answered.

I missed you.

I missed you.

I missed you.

I missed you.

A spring passion that turned into a summer love. A chance meeting that must have been arranged by the gods.

Sometimes in July it got so hot in the third-floor apartment that they had to wait for evening to be cool. But most of the time it was just perfect, sunny and warm with a little breeze through the bedroom, everything just right, everything just as it should be.

She lay next to him on the too small bed, the warmth

171

of satisfaction vying with the warmth of the room.

"I wrote to my wife this week." His skin was damp where it touched her.

She lay beside him, scarcely breathing, waiting for him to go on.

"I told her I thought our separation showed we ought to be separated permanently, that I want to stay on another year, and that we ought to get the lawyers working as soon as possible. Maybe by the time I get back, I'll be free."

"Nice word."

"How free are you?"

"I've never been freer."

"Let me get rid of this." He took the condom to the bathroom and she heard the toilet flush and water run. He came back to the bedroom drying his face on a towel. He had a nice body with hard thighs. Although he had a car, he walked most places. "What are you looking at?"

"You."

"Approve?"

"Uh-huh."

"Need a shower?"

"Badly."

"Let's be good and save on the hot water."

She got out of bed and stood beside him on the thin old rug. He wasn't much taller than she, maybe an inch or two. She had told him she liked that; their vital parts were a perfect match. When they kissed, she scarcely tilted her head. He dropped the towel and put his arms around her, kissed her, held her against him. They were both still slightly sweaty but she felt something like a shiver pass through him.

"I don't know where it comes from," he said, and she

felt his body reaching for hers. "I love you."

She turned so that she could kiss him again.

"I promised myself I wouldn't say that to anyone till I got a divorce. I hate to break a promise."

"I forgive you."

He moved away from her and she could see the sweat glistening on his chest. "Let's take our shower. I have a great ruin for you this weekend. It's across the Rhine from Bonn. A little town called Königswinter. Drachenfels."

"Dragon Rock," she translated.

"It's where the old guy himself slew the dragon."

"Sounds great."

He took her hand and led her to the bathroom. "They don't let you up if you're not a believer."

She kissed his lips lightly. "Of course I believe. I gave you my spare, didn't I?"

They took the Autobahn toward Bonn, the route she had traveled in reverse the night she met him. They got lost looking for Königswinter, found it finally, and saw signs for Drachenfels. They hardly needed the signs. The ruin towered over the town, atop a mountain, one of the Siebengebirge, the Seven Mountains. Along the Rhine were vineyards planted in terraces just like the books said.

A little rail car took them up the mountain and then there it was, just around the corner, what was left from the days of the dragons.

"It really is a good one," she said.

"It really is."

They walked up and around, touched—he had to touch them—and then went back down and over to the lookout point where you could see up and down the

173

Rhine far below.

"We could go to England in August," he said. "See Stonehenge. Have you been?"

"Just to London during spring vacation. And a day in Stratford. The best thing I did was walk up Charing Cross Road from the Leicester Square Station following the flag outside Foyle's."

"What did you buy?"

"*The Oxford Book of English Verse* on India paper with a blue lambskin cover."

"That's a nice way to be extravagant. I bet you read it before you go to sleep."

"Almost every night. With clean hands."

He kissed one of them. "Want to give Stonehenge a try?"

"I want to give everything a try."

"Let's find a place to sleep and then see about a boat ride."

Instead of riding down they found a two-and-a-half-mile walk down the mountain and took it, realizing when they got to the end that their car was parked somewhere far away. It was another long walk to find it, but neither of them cared. They found a little Gasthaus and checked in, then had a late lunch in the restaurant on the ground floor. Rich drank half a liter of beer.

"That's why they go to sleep after lunch," he said.

"They go to sleep after lunch because it's tradition. No one ever told them the world keeps moving from two to four."

"You sure it does?"

She leaned over and kissed his cheek. He was sitting at right angles to her, only the beer Krug in front of him. The rest of the thick wooden table had been cleared. "It's moving now."

"We could go to sleep after lunch. We've had a long drive, a long walk, we've talked a lot. Would my beery breath bother you?"

She shook her head. He kissed her, and she smelled the beer and wrinkled her nose and they both laughed.

The room was typically German with a double bed made up with tough muslin sheets, two thick pillows, and a comforter that it was already too warm for, although the evenings might be chilly. There was one window, and looking out and up you could just see the ruin of Drachenfels.

"Imagine looking out a window and seeing that," she said.

He came up behind her and put his hands on her shoulders. "You don't have to imagine it. It's right there."

"And it's ours."

"Ready for that little nap after lunch?"

He used a condom as he had every time. He had said he would find a gynecologist at the army base who would see her as a favor, but somehow it never happened. A soldier he knew bought the condoms for him at the PX, good American ones, he said, showing a flair of patriotism. She wished aloud once that he didn't have to use one, but he said nothing doing.

The bed with the view of Drachenfels was the best they ever made love on. Something about that afternoon was deliciously erotic. The curtain was open and the shade up, and a glance to the side took in the ruin. They had not made love in a hotel before and from time to time, on the other side of the locked door, footsteps would go by or a voice would call down the hall as she

175

tasted his beery kisses, felt his hands on her naked body, touched his with fingers and mouth.

He reached for the flat little package on the night stand (with a chamber pot in the cabinet) and she said, "Not yet," and sat up to touch, to taste one last time. A child ran down the hall outside the room, giggling, and she thought it was the most exciting, the most arousing sound she had ever heard. She said, "Rich," and lay back on the thick pillow, her hands on his thighs as he knelt between her legs. She heard the package tear — funny how such a mundane sound could take on such meaning, evoke such a strong physical response — and a moment later he was inside her, the child gone, the ruin gone, the only sounds the ones they made together. That wonderful bed.

After that, like all the good Germans, they slept.

When they were together, there was no schedule. There were times and places, food eaten standing up or sitting down, falling asleep and waking up, a shower in the afternoon or at midnight, but nothing like the rigid structure of the Biehl household. She had enjoyed that structure, counted on its unswerving reliability, but having it lifted gave her a sense of freedom, of independence. They were answerable only to each other and there was so little to be answerable for.

They took the boat trip down the Rhine — or was it up? — in the early evening when it was still light enough to see the shores. At every bend of the river there was a view. Castles were a dime a dozen.

"You're a very impulsive person," she said as the boat glided along. "I didn't think you were when I met you."

"I wasn't."

"You must have been. A person doesn't become impulsive overnight."

"Why not? I was a careful, cautious, plodding, dull academic until I got a flat tire on a lonely road."

She laughed. "Except for ruins."

"Well, I admit to an occasional spark of excitement. A ruin is, after all, a ruin. You act on impulse. It's one of your finest features."

"You won't get all plodding and dull at midnight some night, will you?"

"Pinch me if I do. Look out there, on the river. Those black supports sticking out of the water. That's all that's left of the Remagen Bridge. The rest of it is somewhere down below."

"They must have left those as a reminder. Like the church at Beethovenplatz."

"A country of reminders. You cold?"

It was breezy on the water. "It's just perfect."

"Just perfect," he repeated. "I think if my wife had said that once during my marriage, I'd still be with her."

"No, you wouldn't."

"What makes you such an expert on my marriage?" He messed her hair and rubbed her cool, exposed arm.

"What makes people marry," she said, not as a question.

"When I met you, you asked what made people divorce."

"Maybe the answer to one is the key to the other."

"And maybe there are no answers and no keys, just questions and lots of pseudscientific theories that add up to nothing." He looked out over the water. The boat had turned around and was heading back, giving them a view of the opposite bank. They were just passing through what was left of the Remagen Bridge. "There's another side to my marriage, you know. My wife complains about me. There are things about me that irritate her, things I do she wishes I didn't and things I don't do she wishes I did."

"I didn't ask you, Rich."

"I know you didn't, but I'm telling you. I'm giving it to you for nothing. I didn't marry her because she looked good on paper. I married her because that little something inside me said I should. The little something was wrong."

"You changed. She changed. The times changed."

"I think she changed. But she'd tell you a different story."

"She won't get the chance."

"Would you marry someone because he looked good on paper?"

"Not since I met you, since I feel this way about you."

"You mean because we're good in bed? You make it very easy for me to be good to you. Plenty of men would be good to you. If you let them. If I let them."

"I'll never marry anyone who doesn't love a ruin. End of conversation."

"End of history lesson," he said. "Let's go somewhere and drink a lot of wine when we get back."

It was late when they returned to the Gasthaus. They had to ring a bell to get in the front door, and the woman who opened it for them was in her bathrobe and looked half asleep. Rich apologized and she gave them a quick smile, locked the door, and disappeared.

They went up the stairs and found their door. It unlocked with a large, old-fashioned key. Inside, the curtain was still open and the light from the night sky made the white of the bed starkly visible. He put his arms around her and kissed her. The scent of the wines they had drunk was all around, light as the German wines are light, and just as sweet. She felt intensely aroused, as she had in the afternoon, aroused and more.

"I love you," she said.

"I know you do. *We* do."

"I've been thinking all day that I'm here in this little town on the Rhine and I'm with someone I love and I don't believe it."

"Why don't you believe it?"

"Because it's too good to be true."

"Nothing is too good to be true." He started to undress her. "Don't," he said as she opened her belt. "Let me do it. I want to touch you when I take it off." A finger down her breast to the nipple.

"Rich, what you said on the boat, about our being good together in bed. That's not why I love you."

"Forget that I said it."

"It's why I enjoy you. The love is everything else."

"Do I look good on paper?"

"I don't know. I never put you on paper." She stepped out of her sandals, completely undressed now, and stood so their bodies just barely touched.

"Get in bed," he whispered, kissing her. He went to the dresser and she heard the zipper on the kit he used for his shaving things and toothbrush and other necessities of life. He rummaged through it and then said, "Shit," almost under his breath. He came back to the bed and said, "Lee."

"It's OK."

"It's not OK. I'm out. I'm sorry. I thought I had a

179

couple more."

"It doesn't matter. I'm sure it's OK."

"I can't take the chance."

"You're not taking a chance. I am and I'm sure it's OK."

"I don't know." But he was lying down beside her.

She reached for him and said it again, "I'm sure it's OK, Rich," and after that, neither of them said much of anything.

Chapter Six

I'm sure it's OK.

It was the first thing she remembered when her period didn't come. *I'm sure it's OK.* I said it and I'm responsible.

The panic came and went in waves. It was a special kind of panic. She could see that it would make sisters of women who could not even be friends. She was able to quell her fears for several days. She had never been like clockwork, and there were plenty of reasons for her cycle to go astray—emotional reasons. Her last one had been late, too, she remembered, back in June. She would be patient and calm. She would not alarm Rich. In a few days, everything would be back to normal.

She saw him once during that time and he asked her. It was the only time she ever lied to him. It scared her that she would lie and it scared her more that with each day nothing happened. It was near the end of July now and they were planning to leave Germany together on the first of August for a trip to England. She had already written her parents that she was staying on for a second year but would be spending it in Frankfurt.

Now she had this other to contend with. She couldn't travel with him for a month or more—the fall semester didn't begin until November second—and keep this a secret. Nor could she continue to lie. She was supposed to drive down on Friday, taking her belongings with her, to make the move to Frankfurt. They would leave for England a few days later. By Friday her period would be ten days overdue. By the weekend, if it didn't come, she would have run out of excuses. *I'm sure it's OK.* She had done this to herself. Two days until Friday.

Thursday evening the phone rang. Marlies ran to answer it—Robert called nearly every night—and she talked and laughed a moment before calling Lee to the phone.

"Your cavalier," she said, smiling brightly. "He's so sweet, Lee."

She picked up the phone. "Hi. Marlies tells me you're very sweet."

"I'm all whipped cream. How are you?"

"Fine. I'm nearly packed."

"Can I ask you to hold off this weekend?"

"What do you mean?"

"An unexpected inconvenience. I'm calling from downstairs. My wife turned up on my doorstep this afternoon."

She felt suddenly dizzy, as though she had stood up too fast or taken a ride on a speeding carousel. "I don't understand," she said, although she understood perfectly. His wife had appeared on his doorstep, suitcase in hand. She was now in his apartment, *in his apartment.* She was living with him again.

"She got my letter," he said. "I had told her I was leaving here the first of August, and she decided to see me before I took off."

"How long—how long is she staying?"

"I don't know. As short a time as I can make it. If I can

manage it, I'll drive up for a day to see you."

"OK."

"It came out of the blue, Lee."

"I know it did. I'm just unhappy that I won't be seeing you."

"So am I. It's going to work out. It's just a matter of a few days."

"OK."

"And then we'll be together for a long time."

"OK, Rich."

She went to the living room where the Biehls were gathered before the television set and spoke to them. Of course she could stay another week. Don't even bother to ask.

She went upstairs and sat on her bed and felt awful.

She needed to talk to someone. Marlies was too young and Frau Biehl was her mother's generation. But Sally was there and Sally was as savvy as anyone Lee had ever met. She would tell Sally and Sally would help her. Sally would know what to do. Sally would be a comfort.

But for the first time all year Sally failed to show at the Mensa or the café on Monday, Tuesday, or Wednesday. She hadn't mentioned taking a vacation; rather she had spoken of continuing her work through the summer. Finally, on Wednesday evening, Lee called her and they met the next day for lunch.

Dear Sally, she thought afterward. How grim she had looked that day she told Lee that Sam was taking Wendy and going back to the States. And that was it. The only comfort she could reach for was gone.

She left the café and walked up to the castle. There

were huge old trees on the grounds and no one around. She sat with her back to one of the trees and allowed herself to cry. She stayed for a long time, thinking, trying to work out a solution to what was essentially unsolvable. When the tears had passed, she tried to read, but it was impossible to keep her mind on the book and off her problem. It was a week since Rich's wife had arrived. He had called once more to ask her to be patient. But there was no word on when his wife was leaving. No indication. Nothing.

She could not return to the States pregnant. For her parents, for her grandparents, it would be unimaginable. She pressed her German tissue to her eyes and suppressed a sob.

"Fräulein?"

She looked up. A man was standing in front of her. As she raised her face, he squatted.

"Is something wrong?" he asked anxiously.

"No, I'm fine. Thank you very much."

"May I accompany you home?"

"No. I'm really quite fine. Thank you."

The worried face continued to look at her.

She smiled. "I'm all right. Really."

He smiled back in a forced way, then stood. "I wish you a good day," he said and walked away.

She watched him go. He looked back once and she smiled again. It was five o'clock and she would have to start back to the Biehls'.

She had just passed the long street that led to the railroad station and was on the last lap of her walk home when she heard a horn. She looked down the street and saw Rich's car approaching. He pulled to the side, mounting the curb to get out of the traffic lane, and opened the passenger door. She scrambled in and they kissed, held each other, kissed again.

"You didn't tell me," she said.

"I slipped out this morning and called from the post office. You had already left the house. I thought I'd take a chance. I've been talking to Frau Biehl on and off for six hours. Thank God she takes a nap. They invited me for dinner. I don't like the way you look."

"I miss you."

"I don't know how long Marilyn's going to stay. She's being difficult and I'm trying not to rock the boat. I have to get back now. I don't want her to know there's anyone in my life. She's being unreasonable enough as it is. I just wanted to see you this afternoon."

"I'm sorry I left the house so early."

"It's not your fault. I should have figured this out ahead of time. I'm really not thinking straight." He looked at his watch. "I told her I had a meeting at the university, but it looks like I won't be home till seven."

"I'm glad you came."

"It won't be long. She has a job to go back to. I think.

"What did she say about the divorce?"

"She's not making much sense at this point."

"I love you, Rich."

"I love you too. It'll work out. Soon."

They kissed and she got out of the car. She threw him a kiss and watched as he turned left toward the railroad station and the road to Giessen.

She never saw him again.

"There you are," Frau Biehl said as she walked into the house. "You just missed Mr. Singer."

"I saw him downstairs. Thank you for being so kind to him."

"That is a good man, Lee. I'm not your mother, but I can tell you as the mother of daughters, that is a good man. And interesting. I enjoyed listening to him. Smart. You don't find a man like that every day of the week."

"Are the girls home?"

"They're upstairs."

"May I speak to you privately?"

"Is something wrong?"

"Yes."

Frau Biehl's face started to look like the face of the man on the castle grounds, worried and tight. "Come with me, child." It was the first time she had ever called Lee that. "Into my husband's study."

They went in and she closed the door. There were two easy chairs there which, Lee thought, must never have been used. The room was a study, not a consultation room. They sat in the chairs.

"What is it?" Frau Biehl asked.

"I'm pregnant."

"My goodness." Her head dropped for a moment. Then she straightened herself out. "His child."

"Yes."

"Does he know?"

"No."

Frau Biehl shook her head. "Can you tell your mother?"

Lee started to cry and shook her head. "No," she said softly.

186

"I feel honored that you can tell me."

"Rich is married, Frau Biehl. He's been separated almost a year, but it'll be a long time till he gets divorced. This is not his fault; it's mine. I have to decide what to do."

"And have you decided?"

It had come to her at the castle, sitting with the book she could not read and thinking about the problem she could not solve. For no reason she could think of, her mind began to wander to Frau Möck and little Simon Mandelbaum. A matter of trust. A man had entrusted his child, the only thing he had in the world and the most precious, to a woman who for all practical purposes was a member of the enemy but who showed him one moment of character, one moment of compassion, one moment of courage. It had been the smartest thing the man had done in his life.

"I would like you to adopt my child and raise it, Frau Biehl. If you think you can," she said, understanding what she was asking, understanding what it would mean in this family of nearly grown children to start again with an infant.

To her surprise, she saw tears form in Frau Biehl's eyes. "My lost child," she said faintly. She sat quietly in her chair, looking downward. When she raised her eyes, it was to look out the window toward the patio. Her face had a frozen look.

It was one of the few times in her life that Lee wondered what another person was thinking. Was Frau Biehl thinking that this was a Jewish child she was being asked to raise? Was some deep feeling that had been long suppressed emerging now to make the child unacceptable? How does one ever know, how can one ever be certain of another person's feelings? What had Simon Mandelbaum's father thought in that brief time when he was packing the boy's suitcase?

"I would like to have that child," Frau Biehl said finally, still looking out the window, her face still the same mask, and Lee felt the first ray of hope, the first possibility that there might be a way out. Frau Biehl turned to face her. "I must talk to my husband. But I must ask you to make me a promise. You must not talk to anyone about this, especially not to my daughters. Ever. Even after I am dead."

"I promise."

"Go upstairs and rest. We will speak again." She looked at her watch. "Supper will be at seven."

"Thank you." Lee left the study but Frau Biehl remained where she was, sitting in the chair and looking out the window as Lee closed the door behind her.

They passed through an ordinary supper with ordinary chatter. The doctor commented generously on Rich, with whom he had had dinner that afternoon, an unexpected pleasure. Marty talked about her upcoming trip with school friends. Marlies talked about Robert. Very ordinary, very usual.

The next morning Frau Biehl told Lee she had an appointment at Dr. Biehl's office at four o'clock. Frau Biehl came down from her nap at twenty to four and they left the house together.

Dr. Biehl spoke to her alone in his consultation room. He held her hand and comforted her. He had made an appointment for her to see an obstetrician at five that afternoon; his wife would accompany her. As she rose to leave, he shook his head and said, "You should have been more careful," as though he were a friend, not a stand-in for a father.

"I know," she said and he patted her shoulder.

The obstetrician was not as kind and said almost nothing during the entire visit. He spoke more to Frau Biehl than to Lee. She decided she hated him but she kept quiet. Expressing her feelings required more freedom than she now possessed.

When they left the obstetrician, they walked back to Dr. Biehl's office. It was nearly six o'clock and his office was empty. Frau Biehl knocked once on his door and they entered after his call.

"Sit, sit," he said, hurrying to arrange two chairs. He settled behind his desk. "I have just spoken with Dr. Hoffmann. He assures me you are in good health. We will, of course, wait for the test to confirm that you are pregnant and then, if you agree, we will do the following." He sat back in his chair and took a breath. "We have a friend with a small vacation home on the North Sea. The air is very good there, and in general it's a healthy place to live. You will go there immediately. If your pregnancy lasts through the early, dangerous months, my wife will join you. That would be about, say, October or November. We will tell Marie-Luise and Martina that Mummy is pregnant and must rest in a special home because of complications. That is not out of the ordinary, especially for a woman past her thirties. A friend who is a lawyer will draw up the papers, and when you give birth, we will adopt your baby. Of course, we will pay all the expenses of the confinement as if it were my own wife. How do you feel about it?"

"Very grateful."

189

"I think I should add a few things, Franz," Frau Biehl said. She turned to Lee. "You understand we will raise this child as a Catholic."

"I understand."

"No more and no less religious than we are, but a Catholic. And the child will be ours. You trust us with the child and we trust you with the secret. You will out-live us by many years, Lee. I must have your word— which I cannot enforce—that my daughters will never know that this is not the natural child of their parents."

"They will never hear it from me."

"As for Mr. Singer, you will have no need to tell him. If he calls here, I will tell him you have left, gone home. Does he have your address in the States?"

"No."

"That's good." She nodded thoughtfully. "You and I will spend many months together this winter," she said. "Will we still be friends when it's over?"

"I'm sure we will."

"I think the same thing. I think we will always be friends. I am very fond of you. Are there any questions we haven't answered?"

"Only one." She swallowed hard, afraid of losing her composure. "May I visit in future years?"

There was a chorus of "naturally" and "of course."

"You're part of our family," Dr. Biehl said. "You'll be the American aunt with her new fashions and happy stories."

"Thank you."

"There is no need to thank us," Frau Biehl said. "We will always be grateful to you. We look forward to your gift to us."

She left for the north two days later, kissing the sisters good-bye as though she were leaving the country. It was a pleasant drive and the little cottage, while sparely furnished, was more than adequate. The only heat, she noticed as she looked around, was a tile stove built into one corner of the small living room. The tiles were pretty and, she thought, probably hand-painted. She would learn to make a fire, learn to keep house. Dr. Biehl had given her traveler's checks for housekeeping money, and on the first day she found the bank in town, cashed a hundred-mark check, and bought some necessities. There was a doctor she was to see and she called from the post office and made an appointment. There was no telephone in the cottage.

When she was settled, she took the last of her Fulbright money and drove to Puttgarden where she took the ferry to Denmark for a holiday. It made August pass very quickly.

Frau Biehl wrote her one long, informative, encouraging letter a week and Lee answered, addressing her letter to the doctor's office. Often, when she finished a long walk in the healthy German sea air, she would write an imaginary letter to Rich. Once or twice she wrote a real letter, or started one, but she threw them away. They never quite said the right thing anyway.

Her parents wrote to her at the cottage, and she wrote the small part of the truth that they were privy to, stories of seeking out folklore, of learning a new dialect. She had written them postcards from Denmark, so they knew she had taken a vacation. It amazed her how easy it was to deceive them.

The obstetrician was a kindly old sort, and although

she had little confidence in his knowledge of modern medicine, she liked him. The visits were not unpleasant and her health remained good. Perhaps, she thought, there was something to sea air after all.

Frau Biehl arrived in mid-October, after the "dangerous months" were over, and on that day their friendship began to grow deeper. Frau Biehl took over the running of the house as though it were a profession. It had to look just so. Dinner had to be served at midday and a nap had to follow. She served *Quark,* a yogurt-like substance, for supper because it was so *gesund,* so nourishing. She used the word *gesund* at least half a dozen times a day.

When they were not eating or sleeping or cooking or cleaning up or out walking in the wind, they talked. Frau Biehl told stories of her childhood, the story of how she met her husband, and always, recollections of the war. Somehow their personalities, which were so different, blended for those months. They were companions, friends, comrades.

The wind was bitter. There were days they did not go out because of the wind, mornings when the car balked at starting. The baby was due at the end of March and in February Frau Biehl began to prepare for the birth. One neighbor had a telephone. Another neighbor had a car. She kept her clothes near her bed each night in case she was called out.

Dr. Biehl visited several times on weekends and consulted with the obstetrician. He was very happy. "My wife suffered a great deal when she lost her baby fifteen years ago," he said to Lee when Frau Biehl was out of the cottage. "A woman never recovers from that kind of loss. This baby has a place in our family."

She went into labor about two weeks early, in the middle of March, conveniently, in the morning. Frau Biehl left her in a chair and went to telephone the doctor. She returned and checked Lee's condition, then went to the second neighbor to ask for the car. When the car arrived, Frau Biehl carried the overnight case and held Lee's arm. She was an enormous comfort, calm, very sure of herself, firm in her directions.

"I wish Rich were here," Lee said, walking to the door of the cottage that had been her home for so many months.

"I know you do. You've been thinking about him lately."

"Every day."

"You've done the right thing, child."

"I know that."

The car took them to the hospital where the sisters took her away from Frau Biehl. She had held Frau Biehl's hand until the last moment, dreading the time she would have to leave her. She wished one person would speak English, but there was no one. Suddenly, after all these months of speaking nothing but German, she was in a foreign country. She let the hand go, turned and said good-bye.

Before midnight, she had a daughter.

They came to her the next afternoon, both the Biehls, smiling and happy, with a lawyer. The agreement was impossible to understand — she wondered if it would have been any clearer in English — but it didn't matter. She had promised and this was the contract that made the promise binding. She signed and the lawyer left the room with Dr. Biehl.

"She's as beautiful as any baby I've seen," Frau Biehl said.

"Yes. They brought her to me this morning. I touched her." She felt suddenly low, rock bottom, suddenly unsure of herself, of her feelings, of her future, of this decision she had just put in writing.

"It's all right, child," Frau Biehl said, patting Lee's hand. "Rest. I won't leave you now."

"Thank you." She shifted painfully on the bed. "I want to ask you something. A favor. You don't have to do it but—"

"What favor?" Frau Biehl asked gently.

"If you could name her Tina. I've been thinking of names. Tina sounds the same in German and English. I would like—I know it's your choice—"

"Tina is a good name." Frau Biehl nodded her head thoughtfully. "We could name her Christine and call her Tina. Yes." She smiled. "We will do it. My husband will agree to that. Rest now. It's time for your afternoon nap."

Chapter Seven

It had grown dark. The telling of the tale had taken longer than she had expected. Rich had asked questions; at various times he had stopped her and asked her to review things she had already said. At one point he had left the room and not returned for ten minutes. Now he stood at the window, not looking out at the night sky, just standing, looking worn and tired, an older Rich.

"And you went home," he said finally.

"In April. They hired someone to stay with me till the doctor said I could travel. They were afraid I might become depressed."

He looked around the office as though the answers to his unasked questions might be somewhere in the wall of books. "I wish I'd known," he said. "I wish you'd told me."

She shook her head. She would have to say it in a moment, tell him the last brief chapter, even if he didn't ask.

"I tried so hard to find you."

She felt tears spill over. She turned her head and looked in her bag for a tissue. He would ask now, now that she had heard the only thing she really cared about. *I tried so hard to find you.* When she looked up, he was watching her.

"Why now?" he said, and she thought: he knows. I don't really have to tell him. I don't really have to say it out loud. "You could have found me ten years ago. Or twenty. And the hell with your promise. They had no right to ask that of you anyway, that you wouldn't tell me."

"Tina died three weeks ago today."

He whispered something she could not hear and turned toward the window. She started to get up, wanting to walk over to where he was, to comfort him, to receive the comfort that his grief would give her, but she stopped before she had risen. It was too late for comfort, years too late, decades too late. They were strangers who had once shared something, but the statute of limitations had run out. They weren't lovers anymore; they were just people who had once known each other.

"It was one of those childhood cancers," she said. "I was at the funeral."

He turned away from the window, pushed down one shirtsleeve, and buttoned the cuff. "I am very tired," he said, starting on the second sleeve. "I need to get home." He looked at his watch. "Do you live in D.C.?"

"I'm staying at the Mayflower."

"I'll drop you off."

"I can walk."

"Not in Washington at night." He took a jacket out of the closet, put it on, and took out her raincoat.

196

When she had it on, they left the office. He turned lights off as they went, and turned the key in the outside door. They walked down the five marble flights in silence.

They got into his car and he started the motor. "They asked too much of you," he said. He dropped his hands from the wheel and turned the key. The motor died quietly. "I understand about the daughters, but there's no reason why I couldn't have known."

"Don't be angry at them, Rich. I'm the one who didn't tell you in the first place. They're the ones who said not to tell you afterward. They were very good to me."

"That day I drove up from Frankfurt and spent the whole day waiting for you and then I saw you in the street when I was leaving. You knew then."

"Yes. I'd known for a couple of weeks. I told Frau Biehl after you left me that day. A few minutes later."

"Why didn't you tell me?"

"You were married, Rich. Your wife had moved in on you. There was no chance of your getting a divorce in anything less than a year. The pregnancy was my fault, not yours."

"That's a stupid thing to say."

"I couldn't burden you with it. Not with everything else that was happening."

"Why did you assume it would be a burden?"

"Have you forgotten everything? We were young and poor and you were married to someone else."

"You know I would have helped you," he said.

"I know."

"Didn't you know it then?"

It was too hard a question to answer and the answer

197

was buried in events that had taken place too long ago to reinspect. And it was irrelevant anyway. "We talked a lot about love that spring," she said. "We never talked about marriage. Babies are for marriage. I knew the Biehls would love her and they did."

"I have a son."

"Yes, you told me."

"His mother puts every possible impediment between us."

"I have no children at all."

"But you were married."

"He wasn't able." She moved her hands. "It just never happened."

"They let you see her."

"They welcomed me."

He shook his head. "I don't forgive them," he said.

"Maybe it's me you don't forgive."

"I don't know." He turned the key and the motor started. "Maybe it's myself."

He stopped short of the hotel, where the doorman could ignore them. "How long are you staying?"

"I leave tomorrow."

"It's very late."

"Yes." She hadn't looked at her watch for hours, but a wave of fatigue had hit her as they left his office building.

"Good night, Lee."

"Good night." She opened the door before he opened his, and went into the hotel.

It was past midnight. He had not asked for her last name or for her address. She went to the desk to tell them to list her as Stein on their directory but changed her mind before she said it. The fantasy was over. He hadn't asked because he hadn't wanted to. It was over and what she needed was a good night's sleep. Cal would be glad to see her back. She would work and she would forget and maybe someday she would meet someone else. She was free now, free of the past, for what that was worth.

She went upstairs and took a shower. If he wanted to find her, he knew how.

It was on the plane home that she began to think about Ted. Something she had said to Rich, something she had never quite forgiven herself for. Get it all over with at once, she told herself as the plane landed. She took a taxi home, got the mail out of her box, and went upstairs.

There were no messages on the tape. They've given up on me, she thought with an eerie sense of pleasure, and sat in the kitchen with the mail. There was a letter from Frau Biehl, which she set aside, three envelopes which she dropped, unopened, in the garbage, and a letter from a man she knew in California. She dropped that on top of Frau Biehl's letter, washed up, and left the apartment.

Ted Linden's office was still listed at the same address downtown that he had used for years. The subway took her down and she walked the few blocks to his building from memory. It was nearly four when she got off the elevator. He would not be happy to see her. He never had been, although she had asked nothing of him when they divorced.

The secretary was new which made it easier. Someone was coming out of his office as she arrived, and no one was in the reception area which made it even better. She made up a name and the secretary called on the intercom. At ten after four she went in.

"Hi," she said as he looked up in surprise.

"Get out."

"I need to talk to you, Ted."

"You don't need to talk to me and I don't need to talk to you. Conversation over."

"I've come with an apology."

"For what? For fucking up my life?"

"Yes. For that exactly."

He looked startled, but recovered quickly. "Thank you for the apology, Lee. You are excused."

"I just want ten minutes of your time. You won't have to throw me out; I'll go. Just ten minutes."

He looked at his watch. "Starting now."

She sat, unbidden. "It's about why we never had children."

"I don't need this," he said.

"When you asked me to see a doctor," she said, ignoring him, "and I wouldn't go."

"You wouldn't go because you were a stubborn bitch and you wanted everything that was wrong in our marriage to be my fault."

"There were two reasons why I wouldn't go. One was that I knew I was able to become pregnant because I had already given birth to a child." She watched his face. "The second was that if I went to a doctor, he would know I had given birth and I would have had to tell you. I couldn't."

"You had a child."

"Several years before I met you."

"And?"

200

"And I gave it up for adoption."

"Some guy leave you in the lurch?"

"He never knew."

"And of course, I was so insensitive, so unfeeling, that you couldn't tell me."

"I never said that about you, Ted, and I never thought it. I made a promise—" She stopped. "It had nothing to do with that, really. I could have told you. I should have told you. What I couldn't do was talk about it. What I couldn't do was separate myself from that man, from that time, from all the things that happened that year. So I didn't tell you. And you were right. It was all my fault."

"Why the hell did you marry me?" he asked in a low voice, the anger gone now.

"I thought I loved you. Or maybe I hoped. I'm sorry."

"You want me to forgive you?"

She looked at her watch and stood. Her ten minutes were just about over. "Not really. It doesn't seem to be the season for forgiving. I just wanted to tell you. For what it's worth."

"You doing OK?" he asked.

"Fine."

"How's Cal?"

"He's fine, too. I haven't seen him for a few days."

"He get you in bed yet?"

"Cal?" she said, feigning surprise. "I don't think it ever occurred to him."

She went to work the next day. She got up in the morning, as she had for years, dressed and ate break-

201

fast, went down in the elevator and out into the May sunshine to the subway. She had a job and a business of which she was part owner, duties and obligations, nice checks at regular intervals. She had done it and it was over and she was supposed to feel something, but the feeling eluded her. Everything was concluded but nothing was settled. If anything, things were worse than before. The trip to Washington had stirred up feelings better left dormant. At least she had seen Ted. At least she had managed to be honest, to correct an indecency of her past.

Lisa greeted her with a big smile. "Any more detective work?"

"I think it's over. You did a sterling job."

"I'm applying to the FBI."

"Are you really?"

"Yeah. I called up and asked for an application. If they take me, you can hire my girlfriend to replace me. Think they will?"

"I hope not. I like having you here." She went on to her office.

"Honest?"

Lee looked up from her desk. "Honest what?"

"Honest you like having me here?"

"I love having you here, Lisa. You're the best we've had in years."

"Hah." Lisa was grinning broadly. She waved and left the office.

Cal stuck his head in a little while later. "You back with us?"

"Looks like it."

He shut the door behind him and sat. "Find him?"

"Yes."

202

"And?" He set his ankle on the other knee.

"We talked."

"He leave his wife?"

"He did, yes."

"Any sparks?"

"Just some quiet memories."

"Are you sorry?"

"I think what happened was just what should have happened."

"Welcome back." He stood and started for the door.

"What ever happened with the red barrel and the white bathing suit?" she asked.

"Oh, that one. It dried in the twelfth hour. They shot from seven to nine at night. You'll have to take a look when Bernie finishes with it. It's really terrific."

Chapter Eight

Frau Biehl had written a long and heart-wrenching letter. Lee answered it and wrote to Marlies and Marty. The writing was tough. She sat with a dictionary, trying to frame her thoughts eloquently in the other language, trying to be sympathetic to each of them without saying anything against the other two. It took three long evenings to write the three letters.

The man who had written from California came East on business in May and stayed through the weekend to see Lee. He was forty-seven and very nice and made a lot of money. He wanted her to come and live with him in California. They had met over a year ago in Lee's office and had seen each other several times on weekends like this one. She declined his offer.

She worked hard, making up for the days lost in April and early May. When Lisa saw the application for the FBI, she tossed it in the wastebasket after showing it to Lee.

"They want to *investigate* me," she said. "To be a *secretary.*"

"Then we get to keep you."

Lisa grinned. "Aren't you lucky?"

She had discovered Cleopatra's Needle when she had first come to New York. It wasn't exactly a ruin, but it was old and impressive. And it was a neutral place to meet, neither his place nor hers. A neutral place to talk.

The nearby benches had been destroyed by vandals. She sat on a step along the walk and started to read. Bringing the paper had been foolishly optimistic. She couldn't even concentrate on the pictures.

He arrived a little before eleven and walked up to the needle without seeing her. He got close and touched the stone with a palm, scrutinizing it. A man doesn't change much from thirty to fifty, she thought. I wish I had changed. I wish I had stopped loving him. I wish he would do something terribly cruel or thoughtless, or marry someone and let me know. Otherwise it's hopeless. When I'm sixty-two I'll still have this yearning, this awful wanting.

He circled the needle and saw her, came toward her with that little loping walk of his. The walk and the voice. Is that what you love, Lee, two inconsequential physical characteristics that never made a damn bit of difference anyway?

"It's nice," he said, reaching her. "Old. Washington is so damned new." As though continuing a conversation that had been going on for hours.

"Hi."

"Good morning." They found a tree and sat beneath it, he not quite next to her, but under the same tree. "I called the Mayflower the next morning. There was no Lee Stein."

"I went into business while I was married. It seemed sensible to keep the name."

"I thought you didn't want to be found."

"You didn't ask me."

"I didn't ask a lot of things. It took awhile for my head to clear. I didn't know the doctor had died. She wrote all the details. Copiously. I didn't really want to write to her. After I left you that night, I did a lot of thinking. I felt a lot of things I haven't felt for a long time, and more powerfully. I remembered all the times I called and all the lies they told me. The time I went to the house and the doctor pretty much threw me out. He didn't do it nicely, either. And all the while he knew you were pregnant with my child and he was going to adopt that child. I only wrote because I wanted to find you. It took me days to get it on paper. The language is harder than it used to be. Especially the writing." He looked toward the needle. "She wrote me back quite a letter," he said. "She's a tough cookie."

"That's one side of her."

"I wonder how you spent those months alone with her."

"She looked after me as if I were the most important person in the world. She's had a terrible two years, Rich. Her husband died. Her family is falling apart. If she weren't tough, she would have crumbled. As it was, she's the person who kept me going. Then and now."

"Did you know Tina?"

"I visited every year. I brought her American toys and American clothes. I used to love kissing her when she little. She was so sweet." She looked at him, sitting near, but not next to her, under the same tree.

"It's nice to raise a child," he said.

"I wish I'd been able to." All those pretty dresses with expensive labels meant for doting grandmothers. "We all agreed that she looked like Frau Biehl but really, she was a good mixture of both of us. Your eyes and my mouth. And she was tall. I remember once—"

"Go on."

"I can't. I'm sorry." The magazine flapped open beside her and she closed it and rested her bag on it, taking more time than she needed. "She was very pretty and very bright. The school told the Biehls she was certain to get a one in her exams and she could go to any university in the country. She didn't live long enough."

"But she got the one."

"Oh yes. She got the one."

"I left teaching when I came back," he said. "They had a slot for me at B.U., but I'd lost interest. I worked at different kinds of things for a while. Then I went to Washington, worked on a campaign. Met the guy who's my partner and we went into business together."

"What do you do?"

"We publish a group of newsletters, statistics you wouldn't be interested in, but a lot of people are. Current facts. We started with one and kept expanding. We do a lot of special orders, too. Guy calls up and needs some information. We get it, print it up for his meeting."

"I thought you'd teach forever."

"I thought you'd keep working on your folklore."

"I changed everything when I got back. The way you did."

"It's true. That's exactly what I did. And never went back."

"I talked to my ex-husband after I got back from Washington. I told him I'd had a child once. Looking back on it, I realize I could have said just as much to him a long time ago."

"He didn't need to know."

"He did. We wanted children and I couldn't get pregnant. He asked me to go to a doctor but I couldn't because . . ." Because it meant thinking of Tina and thinking of you. Because I was afraid it would mean disclosing what I could never talk about.

"I understand. Sometimes it reaches out with claws to hurt you and sometimes it wraps itself around you to keep you warm." He looked at his watch. "Could I interest you in lunch?"

She got up, gathering the papers. "Lunch, a walk, a crossword puzzle." Rising, she felt lighter.

"Let's start with lunch. I was up early to catch the plane. I have a breakfast meeting tomorrow in New York."

They started toward Fifth Avenue, walking slowly.

"Rich, I want to put it behind me. I don't mean forget. I mean put it in its proper place." She wondered if she was addressing herself. "Tina was a happy experience for me until two years ago. I want to remember her that way, the happy way. You were—you were the happiest experience of my life, but it was a long time ago. I've lived half my life since then. Right or wrong, what's done is done. I'm forty-two years old now. I want to stop looking backward." They stopped for the red light at Fifth and Seventy-ninth.

"Are you telling me you don't want lunch?" He took the papers from her and tucked them under one arm.

"I never turn down lunch," she said. "You know that."

"I don't know that at all," he said. The light turned green and they started across Fifth. "I don't think I know anything about you."

* * *

210

"We don't always do those father and son things. Sometimes he comes to the office on a Saturday and we work together." They had found a restaurant that served Sunday brunch and didn't require a tie and jacket. "He likes what I do. He finds it interesting. I'm grateful for that. We get along. I can't ask for much more."

"Does he look like you?"

"A little. I think he'll be taller when he finishes growing."

"How long have you been divorced?"

"Four years. Five. Should have been longer, but I knew I'd have to give up Jay. She doesn't like me to call him that. His name's Jason. She's that way about a lot of things. It'll change soon. He starts college a year from September and when he's eighteen he can do what he wants. Or such is my fantasy. What's yours?"

"The fantasy was to have a baby but I married the wrong man for that. The plan is to work another few years and see if Cal wants to buy me out. My share ought to be worth half a million by then. The office alone is probably worth that. I've saved a lot, I own my apartment. When it comes down to dollars and cents, I really don't need much. I could take a year or two off without any trouble. I'd like to see the rest of the world — China, Australia. Then come back and do something completely different. Cal and I started that company with a couple of tape recorders. You should see our payroll today, our equipment. I'd like to do it again with something else."

"Maybe Cal was the man you should have married."

"I don't think so, although he'd probably like to give it a try. We're friends and we get along but it's not marriage-making. I think I could enjoy him for a while but I

211

don't think it would endure."

"What would make it endure?"

"If I knew, I'd be doing it."

"I never liked New York." He was still carrying the pieces of the *Times* and they were still walking down Madison Avenue, way down, into the Twenties now, a mile past the glamor. "So damned ugly, most of it. I liked Boston and Washington, baked beans and cherry blossoms. Frankfurt was a nice town."

"You wouldn't like it anymore. They restored your old church."

"At Beethovenplatz?"

"They left the outside the same and made it an interfaith center. Or something. I thought the weeds were wonderful."

"You went back there."

"For a day just before I left. That long stairway is still outside your apartment. Nothing's changed except the church, and they did a good job of making the outside look the same."

"Why did you go back?"

"I hadn't been there for twenty years." He was right about the ugly. Down here it was just old, not pretty, not even interesting. "I walked over to the university but all the old buildings look the same and the rooms inside all look the same. Everything looked familiar and nothing did. Frau Biehl said twenty years was the turning point. I guess it is, for buildings."

"I really wish I could forgive her," he said.

They took a taxi up to his hotel and sat in the bar. It was late afternoon and it was a relief to get in out of the heat. They sat opposite each other and drank cold drinks. There was just enough alcohol to ease the tension.

"I've thought of making a change, too," he said. "I can't leave Washington till Jay's eighteen but after that . . . I'd kind of like to buy a vineyard in California and make my own wine. I could even start from scratch, put my name on a label."

"That's quite a change."

"It hardly seems worth doing if you don't do it completely. I did it once. Why not again?"

"Nice to hear someone say that."

"Nice to tell it to someone who doesn't think I'm crazy."

"You're not crazy."

"Will you have another drink? I'm afraid I can't take you to dinner."

"Another drink would be fine, and you don't have to take me to dinner. Or apologize."

"I have work to do for my breakfast tomorrow. I like to sit in a hotel room with a tray from room service and get my work done. It's one of the ways I enjoy being alone."

"Do you ever take Jay with you?"

"She gets hysterical about things like that. She's got a clockwork mind. We got caught in traffic once and got back to her place a couple of hours late, and she'd reported me to the police. Things deteriorated pretty quickly when we split up."

"They did with me, too, but I probably deserved it." She laughed. "I don't know what's so funny." She laughed again. "I walked into his office a couple of weeks ago and

213

he said get out before I even said hello."

"He can't have known you very well."

"On the contrary." She sipped the drink, enjoying it, enjoying the feeling. "He knew me very well, very well indeed."

She had two feelings as she entered the air-conditioned pleasure of her apartment: of having achieved, finally, a certain control of herself that she had been searching for for years, and of having blown it forever with Richard Singer.

It had been a strange ending to an unconventional day. The two empty glasses stood on the table, filling with water as the ice melted. He signaled for the check, paid it, and took a card out of his wallet and tapped it twice on the table.

"You said a lot of things today," he began. "I heard them all. You said I was the happiest experience of your life. I suppose if I could drop a big chunk of time in the ocean, I could say the same thing. Things changed for me after that year. I suppose they would have changed anyway. No one stays thirty forever." He looked at the card in his hand. "I don't drive around without a spare anymore, not even around the corner. And I carry more insurance on my life than I ever knew they wrote a policy for when I was thirty. I have Jay to think of. I have a business that sometimes keeps me going seven days a week. I'm not sure there's any connection anymore between the person sitting across from you now and the one in Frankfurt twenty years ago who loved you. Who loved you a lot." He took a pen out of his pocket and wrote on the card, and she could see herself doing the same thing when she gave her card to Joey Greenwald and Steven Greene, who had never called her.

"There's always a connection, Rich."

"Maybe," he said. "I think that guy I was would have forgiven Frau Biehl. I don't think this one can. This one doesn't really want to." He pushed the card across the table.

Richard Singer, Black and Singer Associates. An address. A phone number. And scrawled across the top, another phone number. Steven Greene had never called her back. After all of that, it had meant nothing to him.

"That's my home number," he said. "It's unlisted and if I don't feel like answering it, I don't. The number at the office has an answering machine which I usually remember to hook up when I go home. Sometimes I even remember to listen to it. I've never done this before and I expect I'll never do it again. I'm not going to call you, Lee. I'm not sure I can tell you why. Maybe it's just a simple matter of self-preservation. Maybe it's more complicated. Maybe I'm afraid of the consequences."

She picked up the card. Something told her to push it back across the table, do it now, make the break forever — *he won't call you*.

"Don't give it back to me," he said, reading her mind.

She dropped it in her bag and slid out of the booth. "Thank you for a lovely Sunday," she said as he slid out of his side. "And for the other, too, the ruins and the good memories."

"Don't thank me for anything. It sounds too much like a farewell speech."

"I don't make speeches."

They walked out to the street where a line of taxis was waiting.

"What ever happened to the boy?" Rich asked.

"I found him the day before I went to Washington. I never heard from him again."

"Give him time," Rich said. "Not everything happens over a weekend."

"Good night, Rich." She got into the first cab and gave the driver her address.

She sat on the sofa with her back propped comfortably against the armrest and the Appassionata playing on the stereo. She had a file full of business cards, most of them from people who wanted to do business with her. Some of them were from men with no business affiliations at all. Give me a call if you're in — fill in the blank with the name of an American city. From time to time she went through the file and weeded out the cards of people whom she no longer remembered, whose faces had faded so completely that they had ceased to exist. She would keep Rich's card somewhere else. Not in the business card file.

Part Three

Chapter One

She spent two hours the next morning watching a one-minute commercial being shot. She didn't like the housewife character. She hadn't liked her from the start, but the sponsor had picked her, and now the director was trying to get her to be something she couldn't be. She felt sorry for the actress. It wasn't her fault she was sexy with a husky voice when the part needed someone fresh and exuberant with a voice an octave higher. Her agent had sent her over because he knew who was casting.

Idiots, Lee thought, slipping out between takes. Closing the door to the soundproof studio, she heard the kinds of sounds one doesn't want to hear in an office. Shouting. Crying. She made her way to the reception area outside Cal's office. Lisa was sobbing and pulling things out of a desk drawer.

"What's the matter?" Lee said.

The girl buried her head in her hands.

"Lisa, talk to me. What is going on?"

"He f-fired me," Lisa said, between sobs.

"Who? Cal?"

Lisa nodded. It had been Cal's voice Lee had heard a

moment before, Cal's voice shouting.

"For what?" she asked.

"I m-made a m-mistake." Lisa started crying again. "I didn't m-mean to. I'm s-sorry."

"Go to the ladies' room and wash your face. Don't come back until you feel better." She went to Cal's door and knocked.

"C'min."

"What's going on out there, Cal?"

"I fired the little bitch."

"She's not a little bitch. She's a sweet kid who works very hard, and we haven't had anyone work that hard since Jill walked out on us two years ago."

"She fucked us up, godammit!" he shouted.

"Just tell me what she did without raising your voice. Your voice carries everywhere."

"She booked a shoot for the twentieth on the thirteenth. They can't shoot on the thirteenth and the twentieth is booked solid. We don't have a crew and we don't have a studio. It's Castleman. You want to lose that?"

"I don't want to lose it, no. But I don't want to lose Lisa either."

"I want her *out*."

"What'll you replace her with? She's twenty-one and she has a spark of intelligence. You'll be lucky to get yourself an eighteen-year-old who doesn't type and who talks on the phone all day. To her friends. Lisa doesn't. And she doesn't write love letters on her electronic typewriter. She comes in on time and she stays till closing. She proofreads what she types. And she doesn't knit unless she really has nothing else to do. She's worth more than you pay her if you want to know the truth. What is it with you? Didn't you ever make a mistake in your

220

life?"

"I think you've lost your mind," Cal said.

"I'm going to my phone and see if I can rent a crew for the twentieth. If that girl comes back to her desk, either apologize to her or keep away from her."

It took half an hour but she got a crew and a studio. They would do the Castleman shoot here and switch one of the others. It was after noon when she went back to Cal's office. Lisa was not at her desk.

"It's taken care of," Lee said, sitting in the chair beside his desk. "I don't want you to fire her, Cal."

He pushed his chair back, got up and walked around the office. "Since when are you Lisa's champion?"

"She's sweet. She's well-meaning. She works hard. She doesn't have a mean bone in her body. I know she doesn't have the class of those wonderful women we had in our first years, but you can't get them anymore, Cal. They stopped existing or they retired or they're running their own shows. What is wrong with you? What's eating you? This isn't our first mishap and it isn't all that serious. What is it?"

He pointed at her with his index finger, wagging his wrist three times.

"What have I done?" she asked, wondering if she had set up the mistake for poor Lisa, if she had had her head so far away that she was starting to be a liability in her own company.

"You know how I feel about you."

She shook her head and said, "No."

"Have felt about you for years. You know what you did to me when you told me about the old boyfriend?"

"That was twenty years ago, Cal. I told you because I thought we were friends."

221

"We are friends. But you went back to see him because you were more than friends. After twenty years."

"I had to straighten certain things out."

"You're sleeping with him now, aren't you?"

"No."

"And it's killing me. I see you every day and I want you. When you left Ted and we had that time together — that was the sweetest time of my life."

"It was a good time for me, too, but it wasn't a forever time. I adore you, Cal, you know that, but I'm not in love with you. I wasn't even aware this was happening. We have to work together. And you can't take this out on Lisa."

"Reinstate her."

"No. You reinstate her."

"I want to leave Amy and marry you."

"Oh, God."

"Don't tell me you're surprised."

"I am. I thought we'd put that all behind us."

"Maybe you did. I only tried to. I've wanted to do this for years."

"I can't."

"Can't or don't want to?"

She had lifted the chair to turn it so she could see him. "I don't want to. I'm sorry. I don't want to hurt you but I can't be dishonest. I want to stay friends. If we can't — I really don't know what I'll do." She rested her elbow on the armrest and her forehead on her fingertips. "I'll figure something out."

"I'm sorry. I shouldn't have come on so strong."

"Why are you apologizing? You're telling me you love me. Why should anyone ever apologize for that?" She looked up at him. "No one's ever been kinder to me than you have. No one's ever looked after me the way you have. And here we are, apologizing to each other."

"Go have your lunch. If you ever change your mind, I'll probably still be here, waiting to pick up the pieces."

"That poor child," she said. "I have to find her."

Lisa wasn't at her desk, and the desk looked exactly as she had left it an hour or more earlier. Lee went to the ladies' room. Lisa was sitting on the cot, her hands in her lap, staring.

"Are you OK?"

Lisa nodded. "I gave up the FBI for him," she said, fighting back new tears.

"I know you did. You haven't lost your job, Lisa. Come with me."

They went to Cal's office and Lee knocked and opened the door. She walked in, holding Lisa's arm and guiding her into the office.

Cal looked up from his desk. He stood. "I'm sorry, Lisa," he said. "I've had a lot of pressure and I shouldn't have blown up. It was a mistake anyone could have made. I've done worse myself. I hope you'll forgive me."

"It's OK, Mr. Crain."

"And I hope you'll stay with us."

"I will."

"I would really miss you if you left."

To her surprise, Lee found herself crying.

"Just take it easy this afternoon," Lee said when they were in the reception area. "Put your desk back together. Calm yourself down. I'd like to take you to dinner tonight."

"You don't have to do that."

"I know I don't, but I'd like to. You have a big date tonight?"

Lisa smiled. "Uh-uh."

"Then you have one with me. Tell your mother your boss is taking you out to dinner. She'll be very impressed—if you don't tell her it's me."

They left the office a little after five. Cal had taken off in mid-afternoon which helped to calm Lisa down more than anything else. They walked west, toward Ninth Avenue.

"Let's try Greek tonight," Lee said. "There's a nice little place somewhere around here. Do you know Greek food?"

"No."

"Feta cheese and great olives. And lamb."

"I don't like lamb."

"We'll find something you do like. There it is."

"It's nice of you to take me out," Lisa said when they were sitting and had ordered drinks. "You didn't have to."

"I'm listening to you and I'm hearing echoes. You don't have to explain. You don't have to apologize. You don't have to take me to dinner. No one has to do anything. I'm taking you to dinner because I dearly want to. When you get to my age—or maybe even your age—you know there isn't enough time in life to make big mistakes. Little mistakes, yes, but not big ones."

"You're not talking about my being fired."

"No, I'm not. I'm talking about a lot of other things. And you weren't fired. We caught that one while it was very small and it won't get any bigger. You learned a lesson from that and so did Mr. Crain."

"I promise I'll be more careful."

"I know you will. So will he, in a different way. I'm going to order a lot of good things to eat — no lamb — and you can pick and choose and eat whatever you want. And I'm going to tell you how to be the world's best secretary."

Lisa smiled and Lee smiled back at her. They made small talk till the food came and Lee explained all the dishes. Lisa tried every one of them, making sounds that ranged from cautious approval to downright pleasure as she sampled each.

"Now here comes the lesson," Lee said. "I want you to stop saying 'yeah.' Ever again. Got it?"

"Yeah."

"That was the last time."

"Right. OK."

"And when you answer the phone, I want you to sound like you're thirty years old and nothing happens in that office without your knowledge and approval."

"You want me to sound older."

"Just a little more formal. And when you go to buy your clothes for fall, dress up a little. You're not a kid anymore."

"Why are you telling me this?"

"I want to keep you, and I want you to be happy."

"You're very nice to me, Lee. You don't have any kids, do you?"

"No."

"That's too bad. You should've. You would've made a great mother."

Should have. Would have. Contrary to fact.

"Did I say something wrong?" Lisa asked, sounding concerned.

"No. You said something very nice. Thank you. Fin-

225

ish up. I've had all I can eat."

There was a message on the answering machine from a friend and one click indicating someone had hung up. Rich, she thought, but Rich wouldn't hang up. Rich wasn't going to call. She took the card with his numbers out of her bag and tacked it to the refrigerator with a small magnet. Then she sat down and read the morning paper.

Cal's outburst and confession had made her feel very awkward. She considered herself a fairly perceptive person. How had she managed to be blind to his affection? She had thought, after the weeks they had spent together when her marriage broke up, that it was over. It had been one of those sudden, needful times, very sexy as she remembered it, something that made her feel good at a bad time. He had gone back to Amy, which was right, and she had thought it was over. Thought wrongly. There had been a couple of other times. He would say something now and then and she would brush it off because they were partners and it was the business that was important and besides, she liked Amy. And she wasn't in love with Cal.

She tried to keep out of his way at work, but he had a knack for normalcy. He didn't seem to do anything different. When he saw her, it was all business with no apparent embarrassment. But she kept out of his way anyway, avoiding unnecessary contacts.

It's what I missed with Rich, she thought, coming home the next day to the blessed air-conditioning and the nebulous prospect of finding something to eat for dinner, a couple of sweet, sexy weeks together. It was a good time but it wasn't a forever time, she had told Cal. I want a forever time, she thought. I want to spend time with you, Rich, and I can't call you. I can't insinuate myself on your life any more than I already have. If you'd wanted to see me, you would have called.

She went to the kitchen and listened to her messages. There was nothing. Clean. Not even one of those horrendous computer calls. She pulled open the refrigerator door and took out the pitcher of iced tea. As she closed the door, she saw the card. What consequences? Call me, dammit, and ask me if I want to see you.

She couldn't imagine what had happened to Steven Greene. She couldn't believe he had been unmoved by the tape. She tried to think of reasons why he had never called her. It helped her keep her mind off Rich.

The card on the refrigerator confronted her morning after morning, night after night. What would be next for them if she did call, which she definitely was not going to do? They had talked themselves out about Tina, about Frankfurt, about that year and those times. They had met on neutral ground and run down the requisite list. Here's my fantasy, what's yours? This is what I do for a living; what do you do?

What's next is what he was avoiding. Consequences. What was all that nonsense about not riding around the block without a spare? *No one* who insures his life for seven figures drives without a spare. What were you telling me, she wondered, that you're not a kid anymore? I don't want a kid anymore. That it's over and done with?

227

I know it's over and done with. But I've seen you again, and there's this thing inside me that wants you. That needs you. That has to have you.

And I'm terrified that you don't want me.

On Sunday she walked to Central Park and over to Cleopatra's Needle. It occurred to her that he might return, too. A nice romantic ending, Rich turning up at just the right moment. She sat under a tree and looked at the needle. She watched the people. She talked to a dog. After two hours, she got up, brushed herself off, and went to visit a friend who lived nearby.

She anticipated, in the second week after seeing him, that the feeling would abate. Like a fleeting desire for some altogether unnecessary luxury, this too would pass and be forgotten. It didn't.

A letter came from Marty. She was worried about her mother, but otherwise, all was well. She had called Marlies twice recently but she and Kurt were so busy with their friends, she had no time for her sister. The words were written with sadness, not rancor. There was no mail from Marlies.

Lisa bought two new outfits that made her look more woman than girl. Now, on the telephone, she called Lee "Mrs. Linden." A certain smoothness appeared in their official communication with each other that was quite professional, something Lee had wanted to establish for a long time but had never known exactly how to accomplish. Lisa seemed happier than before. One of the young actors recording a radio commercial asked her out on a day she wore one of the new outfits and she was all smiles.

The week passed as though it were ordinary, as though all that was required of her was to spend her days working, her evenings relaxing, read the paper, have dinner with a friend, dip into a book, watch a movie on the tube. She did none of them. She answered the letter from Marty; she thought about the Sunday with Rich; she thought about what she would do if she saw him again. They were pretty thoughts, sweet thoughts, more erotic thoughts than she had allowed herself for a long time.

He did not call. He will never call, she told herself. It was his way of saying good-bye. Why had he bothered giving her the unlisted home phone number then? she asked herself futilely. She was out of answers.

She lay in bed on Saturday night, not sleeping, hearing the dull whir of the air conditioner, cooling and recirculating the air in the apartment. If I see him again, she decided, it's because I want to start over. In the nineteen-eighties I want to do what I couldn't do in the sixties. I want to give it the best try of my life.

By the time she fell asleep, it was Sunday morning and it was light. When she awoke, at about noon, she had made a decision.

Chapter Two

She bought her *Times* and went out to eat. If she had a good enough, late enough brunch, it would suffice for the whole day. Two weeks ago today, she thought, sitting at a small table sipping her coffee, the paper beside her, I was with Rich. There were things she could have said, but didn't. Maybe she should have touched him. They had both been so careful not to touch, as though something might have gone wrong between them if they made physical contact. But maybe something would have gone right. Maybe if she had put her hand on his arm . . . We are people who once loved each other, she thought. Maybe we're people who still can.

She walked home slowly, the paper in a shopping bag. The streets had that Sunday stillness. With weather like this, people were away for the weekend or spending the day at the beach. I should have rented a car and driven to Jones Beach, she thought. Get the tan started. Feel those icy waves.

The doorman held the door for her and she said, "Hi, Stanley, how are you?" as she walked into the cool lobby. Her living room was bright with afternoon sun, a little too bright. She drew the blinds to keep the heat out. It was almost four and soon she could open them, see her southern view, look west through the towers of Manhattan and see the sun set over the Hudson River.

She went through the paper carefully, worked at the crossword for an hour. One of the clues was "wealthy" and she wrote in R-I-C-H, thinking it was an omen. He might be out with someone today, some young pretty thing, a type of which there was an abundance in Washington. Then he wouldn't answer at home and she could decide whether to call the office. Or he might be with his son. It didn't matter. She was not a person who could live with indecision, her own or anyone else's. If she spoke to him, she would know. There would be one terrible moment when he would say, *I think its too late in our lives,* or *The distance is too great,* or *I've been seeing someone for a long time and . . .* And when the moment was over, there would be no more questions, no more wondering.

She drank iced tea and waited. The sun moved and she opened the blinds and looked out on New York. It was clear enough that she could see all the way down to the World Trade Center.

At seven she took a shower and washed her hair. She kept it fairly short and it fluffed easily into place with a dryer. She put on a thin cotton robe, went into the kitchen, and took the card down from the refrigerator.

She felt as panicked as a teenager. One thing you learn, she said to herself, is that in matters of the heart, there is no growing up. There is no being calm about love.

She dialed the number he had written for her. It rang ten times and she hung up. Not in or doesn't want to be disturbed. She sat at the kitchen table and tried to think. The machine was going to answer. What would she say?

231

The truth. Say the truth and then wait another two weeks for a call that won't come. The truth. OK. At least she'd know it had been spoken. She dialed the office number.

"This is Richard Singer. Please leave a message and I'll get back to you."

She waited for the beep and took a breath. There was a buzz somewhere and she felt confused. "This is Lee," she said. "I want to see you." She hung up, her heart pounding.

The buzz sounded again and she realized it was the intercom. She picked up the receiver and said, "Yes?"

"You up there, Mrs. Linden?"

"Yes I am."

"Gentleman wants to come up. Mr. Singer."

She didn't answer. She felt disoriented. She had made a phone call and the doorman had buzzed her. For a moment, she wondered what city she was in. "OK," she said and hung up.

She went to her bedroom to find something to put on. Everything in her closet suddenly looked the same and everything was wrong. She stood there looking at the rack of dresses, blouses, pants, skirts, and the doorbell rang.

My God.

She walked to the little foyer and unlocked the door. "Hello, Rich," she said, standing back to let him enter.

"I wanted to surprise you," he said. "But the doorman wouldn't have it."

"You surprised me."

"I needed to see you."

"I needed to see you, too." She took his head in her hands and pulled him toward her.

As they kissed, his arms enclosed her. Then he moved

232

his lips along her face, down her neck, into the V the robe made. He pulled the belt so that the robe opened slightly and he touched her body with both hands, lightly, as though he might be asking a question or learning something. She let the robe slide over her shoulders and fall to the floor. He bent and kissed her breasts, and she took his hand and led him to the bedroom. He kissed her while he undressed, and she touched his shoulders and his arms and his chest as though he were the first man in her life.

He lay beside her on the bed and said, "Do we know what we're doing?" and she said, "One of us does," and he said, "If you say so," and after that, he didn't say anything; he just made love to her the way she remembered being made love to in all the good dreams, all the good times, the good places, dreams you never wanted to forget, only this time it wasn't a dream. She knew what she was doing.

He sat in her favorite chair in the living room and she sat across his lap. His arms were around her, keeping her warm in the cooled air.

"I couldn't read you," he said, and he kissed her face as she rested her head on his shoulder. "The day you came to Washington or the day we met in the park. I didn't know whether you were sealing up what was over or making an offer."

"I didn't know either. I just knew I had to tell you about Tina." She pushed her hand through his hair. "I still cry about her when I'm alone."

"Why shouldn't you? She was yours."

"Where are you staying?"

"I'm not. I surprised myself today. I took Jay home and

233

I drove to the airport and caught the shuttle. I don't have a razor or a toothbrush or a change of clothes. I intended to fly back tonight. I just didn't know how to talk to you on the telephone, and God knows I can't write a letter. I don't suppose you're one of those modern women who keeps an extra toothbrush around."

"I'm not."

"I'm glad to hear it."

"I was on the phone calling you when the doorman buzzed."

"What did you say?"

"You'll hear it when you go back. Did you really think I would let you fly back tonight?"

"I told you I couldn't read you. Anyone ever call you inscrutable?"

"Never." She stood and retrieved her robe from the floor.

"You're very pretty." He stood and watched her put it on and tie the belt. "I'd like to take you somewhere for a few days and find out who you are."

"Am I so different?"

"I am." He went to the bedroom and started dressing.

She followed and did the same, pulling out a pair of old jeans and a cotton shirt.

"You know how to make a good cup of coffee?"

"Frau Biehl taught me."

"Just one wonderful cup. If you wouldn't mind. And can I use your telephone?"

"Here or in the kitchen."

She put the coffee up while he made his call.

"Ray there? Thanks. Ray, it's Rich. I'm in New York and I've missed the last shuttle flight. I'll fly back in the morning but I may not get in till ten. I have to stop at the

234

house first . . . That's all in the ready basket . . . If he calls before I get in, tell Tessie to make any appointment he wants from noon on . . . Fine. And tell her to listen to my messages but not to erase them. There's one I want to hear . . . Thanks. See you in the morning." He hung up and sat at the table. "It smells good."

"It's almost ready." She dumped the grounds and the filter paper—they were the ones she had bought in Frankfurt because Marty said she should—into the garbage and poured.

He took a sip and smiled.

"You could have had it without making love to me," she said.

"It wouldn't have measured up." He put the cup down. "You have pictures," he said.

"An album full."

"Will you let me see them?"

"They're in the other bedroom. You can sit in there by yourself if you'd like."

"Why should I do that?"

"I only look at them alone."

"Maybe it's time we looked at them together."

She got up from the table but he caught her arm as she passed him.

"Is this going to upset you?"

She shook her head and said, "No," feeling it rush back or start anew, that terrible sorrow, that worst of all losses. He let her go, and she went into the other bedroom, her library and guest room. The album, oversized and thick, lay flat on the bottom shelf. When she got back to the kitchen, he had moved her cup and her chair to his left so they would sit together.

She sat in the chair and he rested his left arm on the

235

back of it, barely touching her. Then he opened the album to the first page, the announcement of the birth of Christine Biehl nineteen years ago and a snapshot of a newborn baby looking at the world with wide eyes.

He went through it slowly, looking at every picture, remembering the doctor, recognizing Marty and Marie-Luise, pausing at a beautiful, professionally taken photograph of Frau Biehl and her infant daughter. He moved the album so that the left page was in front of Lee and the right page in front of him. He watched the little girl sit, crawl, grow, stand, laugh, play, model her American clothes. About a quarter of the way through the book, his arm moved from the back of the chair so that it touched her. His hand held her shoulder. Somewhere along the way, tears fell on a page, on some writing, on a snapshot and she said, "Oh, damn," and while she grabbed a napkin to blot them, he said, "It's OK. They belong there," and he waited, holding her, before going on.

There was a wedding picture of Marlies and Kurt with a little sister in front of them, holding a bouquet. Later, there was a pregnant Marlies smiling broadly. At ten Tina sported a sweatshirt with her name across it. At eleven she turned her head so that she looked so much like Lee that it was a wonder the sisters didn't see it.

"They must have been blind," he said.

"She was their sister and she looked like their mother and they never doubted it. She had Marlies's light hair and Marty's skinny body, and neither of them ever saw the slightest resemblance to me."

He turned a page and went on. The family skiing. A summer trip to the North Sea. The bright, shining face in a ski cap, the lissome little body in a bathing suit. The

236

American visitor out in the Biehls' garden, in her thirties now with her husband beside her.

"Did he visit with you every year?"

"He got bored. There were other places he wanted to go. I didn't blame him. He'd go to London or Paris or Copenhagen and I'd meet him there afterward. That picture is probably the last time he went with me."

He turned the page. Marty with a fiancé. Tina with a group of friends.

Lee looked up at the clock on the kitchen wall. It was nearly midnight. He would have to be up at five to make that first shuttle to Washington. She wanted to ask him not to finish the book, to leave the rest of the pictures, the remaining years, for another time. She could feel the panic, the inevitability of the end, creeping up on her. She had managed so well, contained herself so expertly for so long, but in a few more pages it would all come unraveled.

Marty's wedding pictures. Marlies's two young boys with their young aunt between them. Marty's baby. He turned a page. The little boys grew up. Tina developed a figure. Tina in a long dress standing beside a young man. Not so long ago now. A family picture without the doctor.

She put her hand over his and said, "Please," her voice constricted.

He picked up her hand and kissed it, held it, put it in her lap, turned the page.

"She got so thin at one point," Lee said, hardly able to hear her own voice. It was little more than a whisper. "I thought we'd lost her, but she came back. I wanted to leave the studio and fly over and stay with them but I couldn't. There would have been too many questions. I had to stay here and go to work every day and wait for a phone call or a letter and know it was my child and I couldn't be with her."

There was a picture of the two of them, taken last fall. "I look like hell there," she said. She could feel it going, everything going.

"No you don't."

It was the last picture and she had pasted it in the middle of the page, all by itself. He turned the page over and there it was, stuck into the binding, the black-rimmed envelope that had arrived shortly after her return to New York. He pulled it out, turned it over. She had never opened it. He stuck it back in.

"So many empty pages," she said. She began to cry and she knew that this time there would be no end to it. He put his arms around her and she leaned against him, grateful for his presence, for his comfort, for the simple pleasure of being able to share what she had never shared with anyone in this country, in this language. She wasn't sure how long it lasted but she knew that he stayed with her, never moved till it was over. When it passed, she felt more exhausted than she ever had before, emptier, weaker, half asleep.

"Can I get you anything?"

"No."

"Put you in bed?"

"OK."

"Can you get up?"

She moved away from him. "Yes." The album lay closed on the kitchen table between the two empty coffee cups. She stood and he steadied her, put a supporting arm around her. "I'm OK."

He turned off the kitchen light and they went to the

bedroom. "You want me to sleep in the guest room?"

"No."

"Sure?"

"Yes." She pulled off her clothes and fell into bed. She heard water running for a while and then he got in beside her.

The next thing she knew, the alarm was ringing.

He got out of bed and she heard him dressing. He sat down and rumpled her hair. "I'm setting the alarm for ten," he said. "You need the sleep and you can get in by noon. OK?"

"OK."

"Will you come down to see me next weekend?"

"In Frankfurt?"

"Yes, baby," he said, and in an echo she heard what she had asked. Suddenly it was ten o'clock and the alarm was ringing again.

"You OK, Lee?" Lisa asked.

"I'm fine."

"I didn't know you weren't in till a little while ago. I thought you got in early and were working with your door closed and I didn't want to bother you. If I'd known you weren't there, I would've called."

"I wasn't feeling too well but I'm fine now."

"You don't look so good." Lisa looked worried.

"Just a little tired."

"Mr. Crain left for lunch. He won't be back till three."

"We'll do just fine without him."

Rich called at four. "You feeling all right?"

"A little hazy but I'm coming around. Did you get in by ten?"

"Not quite. Traffic was a bitch. Teach me to travel on the spur of the moment."

"I'm glad you did."

"I listened to your message on the tape. Nice message."

"Thanks for being there, Rich."

"You said you'd come down and visit me this weekend."

"I will."

"Can you make the six o'clock shuttle on Friday?"

"Yes."

"I'll be spending most of Saturday with Jay, but he's got a party at night so we can have dinner."

"I can come down on Saturday."

"Come on Friday."

"OK."

"I'll be at the airport as close to seven as I can make it."

"I'll wait."

"Lee."

"Yes."

There was a short silence and she swiveled her chair so she could look out the window. "Should I say it was like old times?"

"Say it was better."

"It was. I'll see you Friday."

She smiled to absolutely nobody. "I'll be there."

Chapter Three

Cal saw the suitcase in her office on Friday. "Off for the weekend?"

"Yes. I'll be back Sunday."

"There isn't anything for us to talk about, is there?"

"No. There isn't."

"Have a good time."

She made the second section of the six o'clock shuttle and landed a minute or two before seven. He was waiting for her and they kissed and went out to the car. The air conditioner blew hot air for a minute, then cooled, and they closed the windows.

"You give up your car?" he asked as they pulled out of the parking lot.

"I never got one. I rent if I need one over the weekend and I use a lot of taxis. One year when I was being especially impecunious, I kept a record of my expenses. It didn't nearly add up to insurance and gas and garaging a car. Ted had one — my husband — but I didn't miss it when we split up."

"I drive mine to work."

"I have a guy who'll rent me one even if he doesn't have one on the lot."

"You take unfair advantage. Hungry?"

"Not really."

"I have a carton full of stuff from a caterer. She cooks for me even when her cupboard is bare."

"Touché."

"I can drop you at the museums tomorrow when I go to pick up Jay or you can stay home and sleep."

"I'll stay home. I brought a book."

"I have a nice cool library you can sit in and you can eat all the leftovers from my caterer."

The house was beautiful from the outside, cool and appealing on the inside. The kitchen was huge with a large table in the middle and all kinds of desirable appliances along two walls.

"I assume they all work," he said off-handedly. "I've never used most of them. Why would anyone need a trash compactor?"

She laughed. "To make it look as though you have less garbage."

"Last week the bag had more bulk than what was in it. Come and look upstairs."

They went up a beautiful, free-standing stairway and turned into a room with posters and trophies and games and books.

"Jay's room," he said.

"Does he stay over much?"

"Now he does. I've been to court on it a few times. She doesn't like to give an inch."

There was a guest room, a large marble bath, and the master bedroom with a little sitting room off it and its own bath.

"It's a beautiful house. What did your wife get?"

"A bigger one. The one we lived in. I gave her the house in return for fifty-two afternoons a year with my son and two weeks in the summer without her supervision. If she moves away from the area without my permission before he's eighteen, the house reverts to me. I get him overnight now and we have two two-week vacations but it's cost me. Every damn thing has cost me."

"But you have him."

"Yes. I have him."

They had sat in the little sitting room adjoining his bedroom. It looked out over a beautifully landscaped backyard, green and colorful in the day's last light.

"I haven't done very well in my marriages," he said. He was sitting in an easy chair across the small room from her. "Two women I thought I loved. Or thought I wanted to live with. I don't know if I would do it again. I need a woman as much as anyone does. I don't mean just to go to bed with. I mean to talk to. To be with. To have. I like looking across a room and seeing a woman there, one who has special feelings about me. But I don't know if I'm resilient enough to try it a third time. At some point in your life, you have to get smart."

"Or just make your choices as they come along."

"What's your choice?"

"To be here today."

He went over to where she was sitting and held out his hand. She stood and he put his arm around her. "Mine too. And having said all of the above, I would much rather take you to bed now than see what Mrs. Rinaldi put together for our supper."

"So would I."

"Good choice." They walked back into the bedroom.

"Lee, is that what a trash compactor is really for? To make the neighbors think you have less garbage?"

She laughed and put her arms around him. She laughed and kicked off her shoes. She was still laughing — they both were — when they lay down on the big bed.

They breakfasted together the next morning although he had told her to stay in bed. Mrs. Rinaldi had baked muffins and pastry for him, and he had preserves and butter and fresh fruit. He brought the newspaper in from the front door and left it for her to read.

"We'll be back for a while this afternoon," he said after she had poured their second cup of coffee. "If you feel like coming down and saying hello, do it. If you don't want to, it's OK."

"Has he met many of your women friends?"

"Some. I don't usually have someone in the house when I'm not here."

"I'll see how I feel about it this afternoon."

He kissed her. "We'll have dinner out."

"Does the dishwasher work?"

He shrugged. "It did last week."

She cleaned up the kitchen, dressed, read the paper, started on her book. The library was a hexagonal room with three walls of bookcases. The shelves were filled with rare, old books, many of them first editions. One group was locked behind heavy glass. There was a comfortable sofa and she spread out on it, leaving her sandals on the floor. She left the room for a bit of lunch at twelve-thirty and when she went back, she fell asleep. When she awoke, there were voices. She listened, sitting in a corner of the sofa.

"Wow, that's good."

"Finish it. It's too much for me. Hey. Use a fork."

The boy laughed. There were kitchen sounds. Water ran. The refrigerator opened and shut. Chairs scraped. The boy and his father talked, laughed.

"We'd better get started," she heard Rich say. "We don't have much time. Put your watch on the table and leave your shoes at the back door."

A door closed and it was quiet. She walked to the kitchen. A couple of empty food containers lay on the table together with two glasses, some silverware, and two men's watches. At the back door, two pairs of shoes stood in line. She could hear their voices outside. Whatever they were doing, they were having a good time.

She went upstairs and found a window in the sitting room that looked down on the driveway. Father and son were washing a car. It wasn't the car Rich had driven last night. It was older and squarer and right now, it was soapy. The boy was scrubbing it with a sponge on one side and Rich was doing the same on the other. Both of them were wearing jeans and knitted shirts. She could see Jay's bare feet on the wet driveway.

There was something touching about the scene. Both of them were working and both of them were talking. Nothing seemed phoney or forced. After a while, with the car completely soaped up, Jay walked away. She could no longer see him. When he returned, he had a green garden hose with water pouring out. He rinsed off his side of the car, shouted, "Look out!" and turned the hose on his father. Rich took it full in the chest. There was some shouting, which she couldn't make out, and then Rich went after his son. Both of them disappeared but the water kept flowing down the drive.

She went downstairs, left her watch on the kitchen table and slipped off her sandals at the back door. Outside, father and son were picking themselves up off the grass, laughing and panting. They were both dripping and grass clung to their soaking clothes. It was a moment when she knew she had missed something in her life. She had produced a child once, but she had never had a family.

Rich was the first off the ground. He saw her and came over, grinning. "Another year and he'll be able to take me." He squeezed the hem of his shirt and water ran from it. "Jay," he said, "drag yourself over here. Lee, my son, Jay. Jay, this is Lee Stein. I'm sorry. I got that wrong. This—"

"It doesn't matter." She held out her hand. "Hi, Jay."

The boy looked very sober. He said, "Hello," and stuck his hand out, withdrew it, rubbed it on his wet jeans, and offered it again.

She shook his wet hand firmly, looking at his face, a young Rich, a more muscular Rich, a face with a little less toughness than his father's, fewer of those lines that add depth and character.

"You left the water running," Rich said.

"Oh. I'll get it."

"Where are the towels?" Rich called after him.

"Inside," Jay called back, spraying water over the car. "Near the door."

"I'll get them." He ran off, emerging from the house with a stack of old towels. Jay had turned the hose off. Rich tossed him a towel, took one for himself and dropped the others near the door.

Lee went to the pile and took one off the top. She started working on the trunk lid, the back window, the bumper.

"That bumper's pretty good now," Jay said to his father.

"Just needed some elbow grease. Throw me another

towel." Rich walked around to where Lee was polishing the rear lights. "This'll be his car soon. Right now, it's mine. Has character, doesn't it?"

"It looks good."

"He'll drive us home in it. Want to come?"

"I'll stay here."

"Were you bored?"

"No. I like your books. I hope you don't mind my touching them."

He glanced quickly over at his son who was squatting to dry the front of the car. He kissed her and said, "I thought you would. Touch them all you like." He walked around to the front of the car which was now glistening in the sun. "You better put some dry clothes on, kid."

Jay laughed. "Or Mom'll haul you into court."

"Not this time." Rich patted his son's shoulder. "Go on. Leave the wet stuff in the laundry room. I'll take care of it later."

"What kind of car is it?" she asked when Jay had gone into the house.

"An old Checker cab. I fell in love with them a long time ago. They stopped making them." He patted the side of the car. "It'll probably outlast all of us." He kissed her again. "I'll be back soon."

They ate out expensively and returned to the house. He unlocked the glassed-in shelves in the library and showed her his treasures. He had American, English, and German editions, beautiful old volumes, novels, poetry, historical works. She pressed one to her cheek and caught the scent of old leather.

"They're beautiful," she said. "It's a wonderful room."

She handed the book back carefully and he replaced it on the shelf. "You're the same person, aren't you?"

"Shouldn't I be?"

"So many people have changed." She turned, looking at the many walls of the room. "I never heard from the man who used to be Simon Mandelbaum. I found him and gave him a copy of the tape and left him my address and phone number and I was so sure I would hear from him and there's been nothing."

"Maybe he wanted to put it behind him. Not everyone in the world wants total recall."

She smiled. "Like me."

"Like you."

"I made Jay nervous, didn't I?"

"Jay's sixteen years old. A lot of things make him nervous."

"I'm glad I met him. I liked looking at him, seeing your features in his face."

"What most of us take for granted. I'm sorry I botched your name."

"You didn't botch it. You called me by my name. I should have dropped Linden years ago. I thought of it as continuity in the company, but it's really a matter of identity. It's a name I borrowed and it's time I gave it back."

"Why don't we go upstairs and forget about identity and how people change and whether the sun will rise tomorrow. We can talk about all of that next weekend, if you'll come down again." He took her hand and they walked to the staircase. "I didn't hear you give me an answer."

"I'll come down next weekend." She went up the stairs with him.

She took an evening flight back to New York after they

had spent Sunday together. He tried at one point to pay for the airfare but she refused to take it. She said she would fly down the following Friday. The week after that, he and Jay were going to California for their first two weeks together this year. By the time they came back, it would be mid-July.

He showed her their newsletter operation when she came down the next weekend, the terminals on which the data came in, the printing facilities. His partner, Ray Black, was there and they were introduced. He looked at her with a flicker of recognition but didn't remark on it.

"Jay wants to publish one of his own," Rich told her while she was looking at some recent issues. "Something to do with the music he holds dear. I'm thinking of staking him but first he has to come up with a mailing list and a dummy of his first issue. My fear is he'll be successful and that'll be the end of his education."

"If he's not successful, he may drown you next time you wash his car."

"True."

"Where are you going in California?"

"Wine country. I'm pretending to myself I'm a buyer. See what kind of feelings I get out there. Have you been west?"

"A few visits."

"Think you'd like to live out there?"

"It's like another country."

"You've lived in another country."

"I was in love then."

"Maybe it'll happen again."

Maybe. They drove out to Mount Vernon on Sunday

after breakfast, then returned to his house. With some beautiful old shade trees, the back was not too hot, and they lay on the grass which had not yet been cut and was long and voluptuous.

"This is what I miss in an apartment," she said. "It smells so good and feels wonderful."

"I'm almost never out here."

"I would be. I would look for excuses to bring work out here. Then I'd probably fall asleep." She laughed. "And wake up with bugs in my hair."

"Come closer and put your head down here." He patted the front of his shirt.

She crawled over and lay across him, half of her on his body, her head where she could hear his heart. It beat quickly, too rapidly for a man at rest. He put his arms around her back.

"I love you, Rich. That's for free. You don't have to answer."

"I love you, too. I love all the nice things you do for me. I never knew this was what grass was for till today. I wish these weren't one-day weekends, but at least we have two nights. If you want to stay tonight, I'll get you to the airport for the first shuttle tomorrow morning."

"You'll be late for work."

"I'll be early."

"OK."

"I'll call you from California if you disconnect your answering machine. I don't want to talk to a recording."

"I'll turn it off."

"It'll be four weeks till I see you again."

"The grass'll still be green."

"Will you still love me?"

"You know I will." She sat and smoothed his hair. He

was better looking than his son. The toughness, the age, added to the face. "I've decided to change my name back to Stein."

"Why?"

"I liked being Lee Stein better than I like being Lee Linden. There's no connection between Ted and me anymore."

"What's our connection?"

"What we feel."

"Why won't you let me pay your plane fare?"

"I come down here because I want to, Rich. At this moment, you're the great pleasure in my life. I enjoy paying for it."

"Are you trying to keep our connection minimal?"

"It isn't minimal. It's already maximal. I told you that. The plane fare is only money. I don't want to talk about money with you. It has nothing to do with us."

She flew back on Monday morning and went straight to work, stashing her suitcase in a corner of her office. When Lisa came in, she went out and handed her a doctored business card. Lee Linden had been crossed out and replaced in ink with Lee Stein.

"Would you order me five hundred of these?" she asked Lisa.

Lisa looked at the card. "Who's she?" she asked.

"She's me."

"Are you getting married?" Lisa asked, bright with excitement.

"I'm getting single. Stein is what used to be called a maiden name. It's the name I was born with."

"Will you be Miss or Ms.?"

"Whatever. In front of Stein, they both sound pretty much the same."

251

Later in the day she called her lawyer and asked him to petition the court to change her name.

Rich called in the afternoon. It was like those days a long time ago, the days she wanted behind her, when he would call or she would call and they would say nothing and feel better for it. She remembered being squeezed into the booth in the post office, listening to that voice.

On Tuesday, for the first time, she called him in the afternoon.

"Do you mind my calling you at work?" she asked when he answered.

"Why should I mind? I call you at work."

"I have nothing to say."

"Those are the best calls."

He called the next afternoon. "If I had to see someone at *The Wall Street Journal* tomorrow morning and felt obliged to take him to lunch, what are the chances you would have a few free hours after that? I have to be back at night."

She opened her appointment book. Something was scrawled in at three. "My afternoon is free," she said.

"How's two-thirty?"

"Fine. Where shall I meet you?"

"At your apartment."

She went out to the airport with him in the evening, just so they could be together another half hour. The taxi that took them was a Checker, lots of leg room in the backseat and two jump seats that they didn't need, a thing of the past.

"It's nice in the afternoon," she said.

252

"It's nice anytime. But you're right; I like the afternoon too. Especially . . ."

"Especially what?"

He kissed her. "Just especially."

She saw him off and went outside and took a taxi home. She smoothed the bed and rinsed the coffee cups and put them in the dishwasher. Three weeks till she would see him again.

Chapter Four

On Monday, she told Cal that she wanted to sell her portion of the company. That she had thought she would do it in a few years but that she had changed her mind.

He listened in a kind of stoic silence and asked almost no questions when she was through. He said he would ask the accountant to give them an idea of the fair value of the company. He wasn't sure he could buy her out but they would work out something.

She said thank you and stood to leave.

"I have one question," he said before she reached the door. "Is this because of the conversation we had a couple of weeks ago?"

"It isn't. I've just decided to take some time off. There's something I want to do and it'll take a lot of time. More time than I can spare if I work every day."

"I'll try to expedite it as soon as possible."

"There's no rush."

A letter came from Marlies. Mummy had had the gravestone engraved for Tina and she had done something terrible. "When you see it, you'll agree," she wrote. "Sometimes I don't understand Mummy at all. Marty and I have talked it over and we feel the same way about it." And left it at that, a small mystery.

Rich called every few days in the evening. Lisa gave her a box of business cards with her new name. Five hundred, she thought. I'll be gone before I use a fifth of them. But looking at her name made her feel good. There was something about the printed word that gave authenticity to an idea, even the idea of one's identity. I am Lee Stein, she thought, and I will do the things that Lee Stein ought to do. Finally.

The letter from Frau Biehl came during the second week that Rich was away. The stone had been engraved for Tina. Each of her daughters had visited once since the funeral. It would be nice to see Lee again. Perhaps before the summer was over, she would come for a visit.

Rich came back and July was half over. She flew down the next weekend. He looked tan and healthy, happy to see her.

"You get one of these?" he asked, showing her an envelope with a German stamp.

"Frau Biehl?"

"The one and only."

"I've decided to go."

"When?"

"In two weeks."

"From now?"

"Yes. Everything's very slow in August. They won't miss me."

"I'll miss you."

"It's almost four months since Tina died. Her daughters have only visited her once. I think she'd like the company."

"I don't want to see her," he said in an argumentative tone.

"I'm not asking you to."

"Can you manage not to be gone over two weekends?"

"Sure I can manage. I'll leave in the middle of the week."

"OK," he said. "Then I'll let you go."

She booked a flight for a Wednesday in the second week of August and reserved a car at the airport. This time she would need one. She would have to see Frau Möck. In the days before her departure, she worked out how she would tell Frau Möck about Simon. Simon who would never come back to her.

Rich flew up the weekend before she left and telephoned Tuesday to say good-bye. It was an awkward conversation. She kept listening for things that he did not say, and there were pauses during which she could think of nothing to say that had not been said before. When she hung up, she packed her suitcase.

She went to work on Wednesday, her departure day, and stayed till four. The plane left at nine-twenty and she should be at the airport at seven-twenty which meant that taking a taxi at six-fifteen would get her there with time to spare. At home, she listened to her messages. There was only one, a man's voice saying, "I'll call again," and then a click. Another nut, she thought, erasing it.

She showered and dressed comfortably for the overnight flight and had a light supper with the last of the food in the refrigerator. When the plane took off, she would go to sleep.

She was dressed by five-thirty and feeling restless. It was time to go. At the airport, she could buy a magazine or read one of the books in her carry-on. She went to the closet for her raincoat and the phone rang.

She was so sure it would be Rich that the voice at the other end left her feeling confused.

"Mrs. Linden?" a man said.

"Yes."

"This is Simon Mandelbaum."

"I — yes, hello." She had wanted to address him by name

256

but didn't know which to use.

"Do you have a moment?"

She looked at her watch. It was a quarter to six. "Yes, of course."

"I listened to the tape last night."

It had been three months since she had handed the cartridge to him in that beautiful living room with all the windows looking out on his lush property. Three months. "Last night," she repeated.

"I'd like to talk to you. I have your address here. I could be at your place in twenty minutes."

I'll miss my flight, she thought miserably, seeing her plans disintegrate, the long weekend visit, the car waiting for her at the Frankfurt airport, a cable to be sent to Germany.

"Will I be interfering with anything?" the voice asked.

"Of course not. Come on over. I'll make some coffee."

"You're very kind."

It was almost exactly twenty minutes later when the buzzer rang. A little more than five after six. Still enough time if he didn't stay long.

She opened the apartment door at his knock and shook hands with him as he came in. He was the same dark-haired slight man she had met in May, dressed in a well-pressed summer-weight suit with shirt cuffs showing at his jacket sleeves.

"I'm very grateful to you," he said.

"Make yourself comfortable," she said. "I'll bring the coffee."

"Thank you so much."

She brought the coffee, poured it, and set the carafe on one of those glass warmers with a candle in the middle which all the Germans seemed to use and which Marlies had sent her for her last birthday. Or maybe her fortieth. The flame, seen through the glass columns, multiplied and danced. It was quite pretty.

Simon Mandelbaum watched it for a moment before he spoke. "I thank you for this."

"What would you like me to call you?"

"Steve. I've been called that most of my life."

"I'm Lee."

"Lee," he repeated. "Lee." As though having trouble beginning.

"Would you like something stronger to drink? Scotch, perhaps?"

"I'm not much of a drinker," he said. He looked at the flame again. "Yes, I think I could drink some Scotch. Just a shot glass."

She filled a double shot glass in the kitchen and brought it back to him. He sipped it once, then again, and put it down.

"I have never really known who I was," he said. "My mother is only a vague memory. There are no pictures of her, of course. Or of my father. For some reason, I have always seen him a little better. He had dark hair. That's not much of a memory, is it?"

"What your father looked like was ephemeral," she said. "What he did will last forever. Your father was a smarter man than a lot of other people."

"That's true. That I am here today is proof of that. Incontrovertible proof." He sighed. "You must have been surprised when I told you on the telephone that I had just listened to the tape last night."

"I was."

"I put it away after you gave it to me. Actually locked it up in the bank. My cousin Joey said not to listen to it, it would bring back painful memories. My wife cried and said why do you want to find out the horrors that happened to your parents? There's a whole chunk of my life, Mrs. — Lee — that comes to me only in dreams, mostly nightmares. Still after forty years. When I'm awake, it's a blank. When you said that name to me, Frau Möck, it was like a blinding flash. Something finally to link me to that time, to give me a clue to myself. I grew up in a strange family in Brooklyn."

"Joey's family."

"The Greenwalds, yes. Joey's a pretty normal man. His sister seems to lead a normal life, too. She does the things that women like her do. She isn't happy, but she isn't unhappy either. But their parents, their parents were crazy, paranoid you'd have to say. Joey's mother wouldn't let me walk to school alone. She wouldn't let me walk home alone. I learned the language and I made a couple of friends and there she was, every day, standing at the gate when school let out, waiting for me. After a while, I wasn't sure who was protecting whom. I've never met a woman who was more well-meaning, but all I ever learned from her was fear."

Through the doorway to the kitchen, Lee could see the clock on the wall. A quarter to seven. She would not get to the airport two hours early, if she got there at all.

He sipped his Scotch again and finished the coffee in his cup. She reached over and poured seconds for both of them. Then she blew out the candle.

"That's very pretty," he said.

"Thank you. It was a gift."

"Every day for the last three months," he said, "I thought about that tape, sitting there, locked away, holding the secret of my life. I would get up in the middle of the night and not be able to fall asleep again. My wife — my wife is the sweetest, kindest person I have ever known, the most gentle — my wife screamed at me finally. 'Why don't you listen to the damn thing so you can sleep through the night?' " He raised his voice to mimic her. "I hadn't even known that she understood the connection. I had thought . . ." He sipped at the Scotch. "So I took the tape out of the safe-deposit box and brought it home. I went into my study last night and I shut the door. I will tell you, I was terrified at the prospect of listening to it. I thought the Greenwalds had saved me. They had rescued me from dank cellars with vermin rustling around where I was put for God knows what reason, certainly not because I had been bad. I hadn't been bad." He sounded as though he was defending himself against charges.

"You don't have to talk about it, Steve."

"I do. I do," he said again. "I spent the whole night listening to that tape. I memorized it. I learned German from it. Do you know, I never learned to speak regular German. I must have understood it once, but my language was the village dialect. I never went to school, you know, not till I came to the States. At home, all we spoke was the dialect. She spoke it to me. Frau Möck." He looked at his watch. "May I use your phone?" he asked.

"It's in the kitchen."

He went in and called his wife, telling her he would be later than he expected. It was past seven-thirty now. He spoke comfortingly to his wife. If she was the gentlest person he had ever known, surely she must say the same of him. He hung up and came back to the living room. "This is a beautiful apartment," he said.

"Thank you."

"What a nice view you have." He walked over to the windows with their magnificent nighttime panorama. "I've always wanted an apartment in Manhattan, but we would never give up our house."

"I don't blame you."

He sat down in a chair so that he was across the coffee table from her. "Things came back to me," he said. "When I listened to your tape, *I saw myself in my father's house the day she came for me.* I saw my father. I had never understood why he sent me away. I remember the walk to her house. She held my hand. It was a big, tough hand with calluses. That was the last time I walked in the street till the war was over. The last time. I never knew until last night what happened to my mother. I never knew anything. I remember when the Greenwalds came and took me away. I was terrified. Here were two strangers who walked into the house and started demanding things and she caved in. It was the most ironic thing you can imagine. Of the three women who were mother to me—I called her Mama, I remember—she was by far the strongest. She was a big woman physically, busty. I remember the costume she wore."

"She was still wearing it twenty years ago when I knew her."

"And the voice," he said as though he had not been interrupted, "my God, that wonderful voice. She was strong as an ox. She did the farming, you know. Her husband had a job in the city. It was the women who did most of the planting and the picking. And there were the Greenwalds, two little people who were afraid of their shadow, and they reduced her to tears. I suppose it was the residual fear that the war had instilled. She had protected a Jewish child illegally. Maybe she thought they would throw her in a camp if they found out what she had done. But she thought of me as her son."

"Twenty years after the war she was still very broken up about losing you."

"I only remember our escape dimly. They kept giving me

261

chocolate and telling me everything would be all right. I had never had chocolate before that trip. Oh, maybe when the Americans came. And chewing gum. I couldn't believe New York. I had never seen a flush toilet before. An elevator. A train." He got up and retrieved his drink. "They really kidnapped me, didn't they?"

"I hate to put a label on what they did. It's really a story full of heroes, not villains. In retrospect, some of the heroes seem less heroic."

"You're very charitable."

"There's no other alternative. Is there?" she asked.

"No. None at all." He put the glass down on the table. "I thought — I stayed up most of the night, listening and thinking about all this — what would there have been for me if I'd stayed, if they hadn't come and gotten me? I could have grown up to be a farm boy or gotten a job in some shop in a nearby town. Instead, I've become educated and fairly successful." He began to reminisce about his boyhood in Brooklyn, the family that raised him, his education, his marriage. He went on with his biographical monologue, hardly pausing, seeming to derive pleasure from it.

"I must ask you now," he said finally, "I feel I have to know all these things — why is it that you waited twenty years to find me?"

"Something happened to me at the end of the year that I was there, something very profound and very personal. I left a lot of things undone because I didn't want to be reminded of what had happened. Recently, I picked up the loose ends."

"I apologize. I didn't mean to dredge up unhappy memories."

"It's all past now."

"I'd better call my wife again."

262

She wished she could get to a telephone to cancel her reservation and see if anything was available for the next day, but the last thing she wanted to do was make him feel guilty about missing her flight. He spoke to his wife for several minutes, placating her. When he was off the phone, she excused herself, went to the bedroom, cancelled her flight and the car and asked for a booking for the next day.

"I'd like to ask a favor of you," the man in the living room said when she returned. "I want to see Frau Möck. I don't know the language and I don't know how to reach the village. I wonder if you would go with me, be my guide for a few days. Do you ever go back?"

She smiled. "I was going to go tonight."

He looked in the direction of the door where her bags were waiting. "I'm so sorry," he said. "I've ruined your vacation."

"Just postponed it. And it's more of a visit than a vacation. I was planning to see Frau Möck myself. You've really given me a reprieve. I won't have to tell her I found you and never heard from you again."

"I'll get us on a plane tomorrow," he said. "If you don't mind."

"Not at all. I think it'll be one of the great pleasures of my life."

Chapter Five

They landed on Friday morning, one day later than she had planned. Steve had managed to get two first-class seats and he reserved a Mercedes instead of the little German Ford she had wanted for herself.

He paled visibly when he came to customs. If he was able to speak German, he did not show it. On the plane, he had confessed his fear of setting foot on German soil, of seeing men in uniform, of hearing that language spoken.

She drove the Mercedes, following the car rental agent's directions to the Autobahn. All they saw of Frankfurt was glimpses of the outskirts and tall modern buildings in the distance. Then, suddenly, there was a sign to Giessen and her own set of personal memories went to work.

"There's an old hotel in town not far from where I'll be staying," she said when the Giessen sign was behind them. "We'll try to get you a room there. Otherwise, there are newer hotels."

"You're welcome to the car. I won't drive here. I've just been watching them. They're monsters."

"But exactly within the law. They never give up the right of way to be polite the way Americans do. But then, they don't expect you to give it up either. They do exactly what the law requires."

"And if the law requires savagery, they give savagery."

"Perhaps." She had not slept very long on the plane and her mind rebelled at thinking beyond the task of managing the Autobahn.

"These people you're staying with," he went on as though he had had sufficient sleep or perhaps just wanted to take his mind off where he was and how it figured in his life, "you know them well."

"Very well and very long."

"And you trust them."

"With my life, Steve. With my very life."

It seemed to satisfy him. A few minutes later, he was asleep.

She got off at the Giessen exit and picked up the road north. It was newly paved but no wider than it had been twenty years earlier. It curved gently here and sharply there. Steve woke up and asked where they were.

"About thirty kilometers away."

This was the road, but she could not put her finger on the point where she had met Rich. There were so many zigs and zags, so many stretches that looked just like the ones before and the ones that came later.

"It's nice-looking country," Steve said, almost grudgingly.

"It's beautiful."

"You're very kind to be doing this for me."

"I've waited a long time for this. It's more than I ever thought would happen."

She saw the castle in the distance and knew they were close. "Like a fairy tale," Steve said, looking up at the castle. "For those whom the law loved. You must be very tired."

"I won't collapse till I walk the last flight of stairs."

He smiled.

She worked her way over to the old hotel. "Stay here. I'll see if they have a room."

She was very tired now, yearning for sleep. The desk clerk was brisk and efficient. She took the best room he had and showed the porter out to the car. She accompanied Steve to the desk and helped him register.

"I'll come back for you at dinner time," she said. "Well, supper actually. Here's the phone number. If you speak English, she'll put me on. Have a good rest."

He thanked her and she went out to the car. In less than five minutes, she was climbing the Biehl stairway, one slow step after another, with her luggage.

They embraced in the foyer and she explained her delay.

"You found the little boy," Frau Biehl said. "After all these years."

"I'm taking him out to the village to see Frau Möck. Not today. We're both very tired. He's staying at the hotel. I expect he's fast asleep already. May I go up to my room?"

"It's all ready," Frau Biehl said. "Have you had dinner?"

"I'm not hungry. I'll wait till supper." She slung the carry-on over her shoulder and picked up the suitcase. One trip up was all she had strength for.

"He's here, you know," Frau Biehl said.

"Who?" She stopped on the second stair.

"Your Richard."

"Rich? Here? He's in Washington. He called me Tuesday night."

"He arrived yesterday. On your plane. The one you meant to be on."

She stepped back down into the foyer and dropped her luggage. "I don't understand."

Frau Biehl motioned with her index finger. "Come with me."

They went into the doctor's study, the room where Lee had once told this woman she was pregnant. Little in the room had changed. Frau Biehl took two letters from the desk and handed them to Lee. They were both airmail from the United States and addressed in Rich's handwriting.

266

"He wrote to me," Frau Biehl said. "Twice. The first time he asked for your address. The second letter, this one," she tapped the one on top, "this letter is for you, not me. What he says in it, he wants to say to you but he doesn't know how so he says it to me. But it's your letter."

"I can't read something that isn't addressed to me."

Frau Biehl smiled. "I give you my permission."

She put the letters in her bag.

"We talked yesterday, Richard and I. An intelligent man. A good man. I told you that a long time ago. We talked about Tina, about politics, about his wife and son. You know he has a son?"

"Yes, I've met him."

"He's a good father to that boy. I can feel it. We had a good time together yesterday, just talking."

"Where is he now?" Lee asked.

"*Ach,* you know where he is. He's a man who loves ruins, you once told me. He's off visiting our town's only ruin."

Lee looked at her watch. "I'll be back," she said.

There was one car, an Opel, parked in front of the ruin. As usual, the wind was blowing. Summers would always have been cool in this castle if its beneficiary had only lived to enjoy them. She walked through the great gap that must once have been a door and saw him, higher up, on the other side, looking out a massive space in the wall. His shirt was rippling in the breeze and his hair also. So many little things about him, the tan on his arm that started at the sleeve of his summer shirt and went down to the line of his watch, the little hairs bleached gold in the sun, the straight line of his body, the strength in those thighs, in the arms. He moved his hand and the watch crystal caught the sun from the open roof and flashed like a jewel.

For all those small, meaningless things you love a man,

267

she thought, and you hope they add up to forever. It's the big things that go wrong, and after they collapse — the big, important, meaningful things — his arm will still be brown from the sleeve down and the hairs will still be gold, and you'll look at him and still want to spend one sweet, sexy week with him before the end comes. But it will never happen. It was too early the first time and too late the second.

"You forget sometimes how much certain things meant to you." He was looking at her across the space that had been a castle. "How happy you once were."

"I never forgot."

He started down the slope along the wall. "It's so cool here, you could forget it's August."

"Why didn't you tell me you were coming?"

"I wanted to surprise you. I wanted to surprise myself. Then you didn't show up."

"Simon Mandelbaum called just as I was ready to leave for the airport."

"The boy from the village?"

"He waited three months to listen to the tape. Then he wanted to talk and I didn't have the heart to let him down. I missed the plane."

"Get one last night?"

"He got us one. I guess he can pull two first-class seats out of a hat when every plane is booked solid."

"I told you you don't play fair. I could have called a senator who would have flown me to Rhein-Main on a military plane, but I decided to play by the rules and be a standby on your plane. About nine o'clock they let me on. It took me awhile to figure out that they gave me your seat."

"I'm glad you came."

"You know," he had reached her by now, descending along the wall to her level, crossing the uneven, rocky, weedy floor, "this is the second time in my life that you've left me alone for a day with that woman."

"She's not so bad, Rich. She's not bad at all."

"I still don't feel about her the way you do."

"You don't have to. You don't have to feel about anything the way I do."

"Are we arguing about something?"

"I'm not. I haven't raised my voice."

"You never raise your voice. It's one of the beautiful things about you. Your voice is always calm and comforting. It's more than that. When I hear it on the phone, I feel aroused."

She put her hand on his arm, the tan, hard arm with the little golden hairs. "You never told me that."

"I don't tell you everything all at once. I save things. I was saving that for a special time. For today. I wanted to tell you that here." He kissed her. "Hello," he said.

"Hi."

"Let me take you back so you can sleep."

"I came in Simon's car. Steve's car."

"Leave it. We'll pick it up later. You look very tired." They left the ruin and he saw the Mercedes. "Classy," he said. "I got an Opel for old time's sake. Putting that car in reverse brought back a lot of old memories. But I couldn't find the place on the road where I met you."

"I couldn't either."

He started the motor and she closed her eyes. When she got back to Frau Biehl's, her luggage was up in her room and the bed turned down. The next thing she knew, it was supper time.

The four of them sat around the dining room table eating a German supper. There was a stack of large oval slices of rye

269

bread and another stack of black; smoked ham, smoked eel, two kinds of cheese, two kinds of wurst, salads she had never been able to identify but which she remembered. And of course a half-pound chunk of butter on a glass dish. For the men there was beer in those bottles with caps held on with metal fasteners, the kind of beer the doctor used to drink at supper in the days when conversation flew around the table, the happy old days.

Rich sat at the head of the table, still dressed in his knit shirt and tan pants. He looked relaxed and accepted Frau Biehl's occasional correction of his grammar in good humor.

"A professor must speak perfectly," she stated, and no amount of explanation that he was no longer a professor fazed her. But she called him by his first name this time. She called Steve "Mr. Greene."

Steve stumbled uncomfortably with the language, requesting help frequently. The German that he still remembered was largely the village dialect. He used the familiar pronoun, as children do, and was embarrassed that he could not speak as a man of his age was expected to. He was an interesting oddity, a middle-aged man with the language of a small child.

Frau Biehl questioned him about his childhood in the village, interpreting his responses and never once correcting him. Finally, she said it was too strenuous a task for him to speak German and he should eat his supper in peace.

The two women cleared the table and the men retired to the living room. In the kitchen, Frau Biehl insisted on loading the dishwasher without help.

"It's good to hear voices in this house," she said, her hands moving. "It's good to have a table full of people. Tomorrow I bake cinnamon cake for you and fruit torte with whipped

270

cream." She sounded excited. "I am selling the house."

"What?"

"It's too much for me. The cleaning woman and I clean all the rooms and no one stays in them, no one leaves a mark. My husband died here, my daughter died here. I will die somewhere else."

"Don't say things like that. You're only sixty-two."

"Already sixty-three."

"Where will you go?"

"To Frankfurt, maybe. Somewhere where I can walk into the city, listen to music, shop at a market."

"You don't want to live near your daughters."

"Why should I do that?"

"Because they love you. They have their problems, but you're their mother. They'll come back to you."

"Never." She closed the dishwasher and wiped her hands on a towel. "You're better to me than either one of them. In my will I'm leaving you my jewelry."

"Please don't."

"Why not? You'll enjoy wearing it. They'll only sell it for the money."

"I want to be friends with your daughters. They're both younger than I. I want to have them as friends for the rest of my life."

"Friendship," Frau Biehl said disparagingly.

"You should think about living," Lee said. "You're young enough and beautiful enough to marry again."

"*Ach,* I've already had an offer."

Lee smiled. "You see?"

"I don't want to marry one of my husband's old friends."

"Then go and live near Marty. She'll find men for you, wonderful men."

"Frankfurt is better."

271

"Why?"

"I can take the train here and visit the cemetery."

Lee turned away. From the living room came the voices of the men speaking English, a house with voices, a house with memories.

"I'm going to the cellar for a bottle of wine," Frau Biehl said. "Maybe you can find the glasses in the dining room. The tall ones with the gold. We should drink a good bottle of wine tonight. That's what my husband would do."

The men started to leave at nine. Steve was tired, nervous, exhausted from his attempts at German. Lee said she would pick him up at ten the next morning.

"I think I'll drive into Frankfurt," Rich said. "See what they've done to my church. Find out whether anyone I know still lives in that house. I'll see you in the evening."

"Tell him he comes here for coffee," Frau Biehl said.

"Tell her I understand German," Rich said in German. He shook Frau Biehl's hand and he and Steve left the house.

"I offered him a room here," Frau Biehl said when they had gone. "He wouldn't take it. He's staying at that old hotel. It's so run-down now, I don't know how they stay in business. He could have stayed here. He could have a bed in your room. I look the other way. I'm a modern woman, you know."

"I know you are. He just doesn't want to be a bother."

"My cleaning woman would polish his shoes if he left them out. In the hotels, they don't do that anymore." She sighed. "Times have changed."

Lee was up at seven, rested and refreshed. Walking down the stairs, she smelled coffee. They breakfasted together in the dining room, Frau Biehl drinking her tea, Lee her coffee.

272

"You will marry him this time," Frau Biehl said.

"Not this time and not any time."

"Ridiculous. Read that letter I gave you. The man loves you."

"The man also doesn't want to marry again. He told me in as many words."

"You listen too much to the words and not enough to the soul."

Lee laughed.

"Listen to me," Frau Biehl said. "I'm not wrong."

"He doesn't need to marry. He has a son. He's an attractive man. He can always find a woman when he wants company, a young woman if he wants."

"You're too smart to say things like that. Do you ever look at yourself in the mirror? You're a beautiful woman. You don't look your age. You have good bones, you're slim like me. Slimmer. My husband wanted a thin wife and I kept thin for him. You look like you did when you were a girl. Not every man wants a young woman. Some men want a woman with character, with memories, with the kind of ideas it takes years to develop. You'll see. Today he'll go to Frankfurt; tomorrow he'll marry you."

Lee laughed again. "You see why I visit you. You're very good for my ego."

"Ego is what you need. Come, let's wash our dishes. I want to go to the cemetery with you before you pick up Mr. Greene."

They drove to the cemetery in the Mercedes. It was quiet and calm and the sky was as clear as she had ever seen it. She felt unexpectedly apprehensive. Afraid was more like it. She would see Tina's name engraved on a stone with her birth date and death date. Christine Biehl. The end. A life come and gone.

She stopped the car and sat behind the wheel.

Frau Biehl patted her arm. "Come, child. No one minds if you cry here."

She got out of the car and helped Frau Biehl out.

"I have done something a little different," Frau Biehl said as they walked. "My daughters are unhappy but whatever I do, my daughters are unhappy. You will understand."

In the distance, the stone looked beautiful, a brilliant white, the sun already on it, a circle of flowers all in bloom, clipped green grass beyond, a private resting place for a noble family.

"Go and look," Frau Biehl said.

She went forward by herself till she was close enough to read the inscription. "Oh," she said. "Oh Frau Biehl." The name on the stone was Tina Biehl. Tina. Etched in stone.

"She was only Christine in her passport and on the baptismal certificate. Even the teachers called her Tina. And it was your name for her."

My name for my baby. "Thank you."

"There's nothing to thank. We thank each other."

"Yes." She walked to a group of trees some distance away and found a small stone. Returning, she placed it in front of the grave and stood looking at the name.

She glanced at her watch. It was ten to ten. There was just enough time to drop Frau Biehl off and pick up Steve.

"Go," Frau Biehl said. "I like to take a long walk in the morning. Go and get your little boy and take him to his mother. It's about time."

Lee walked back to the car. As she drove away, Frau Biehl was picking up bits of invisible debris in front of the stone, cleaning up for her family in her housewifely way.

Chapter Six

Even the road had changed. After they went over the mountain and came out of the woods, there was a new straight road designed, not to reach the villages, but to avoid them. Every kilometer or so a sign with a familiar name pointed to a side road.

"You understand that I am terrified," Steven Greene said.

"I understand. More than you can imagine, I understand."

"I don't know if I'll be able to speak."

"I wouldn't worry about it. Someone will find the words."

"I hope so." He fastened his eyes on the passing scenery. "You and Rich," he said. "I didn't realize this was a vacation you were sharing."

"Nor did I. He came here as a surprise. I thought I was coming alone."

"I gather you knew each other here when you were a student."

"We met the night I came back from the American embassy in Bonn when I was trying to locate you."

"You did that?"

"I was twenty-two and I was so sure the ambassador himself would get on the phone to New York and find out where you were. They wouldn't give me the time of day."

"I had no idea you went to all that trouble."

"It was no trouble. And don't apologize. If not for you, I would never have met him. Here's our turnoff."

Once off the highway, there were cobblestones. It was like an old world hiding at the edge of the new. She made a sharp turn and they were in the village. She put her foot on the brake and looked at the houses on the left side. None looked like Frau Möck's.

"They've changed it," she said with disappointment. The facade was completely different, more modern, stucco covering the handsome old beams. The old windows had been replaced with large, single-pane windows of a type now used everywhere in Germany.

"You're sure that's it?" Steve asked.

"The number is right. Nineteen."

"Do you think you could find number twenty-seven? I think that was our house."

"I'll try." She drove slowly, watching the numbers. Twenty was around a corner. They passed the church. She slowed, stopped.

"That could be it," he said in a low voice. "It could."

She turned around and started back. A group of children were playing in the road. They moved away as the Mercedes inched along. A woman came out and swept her walk. She stopped to look at the car. Lee parked in front of the altered house that had the Möck's number on the door.

"Stay here," she said. Beside her, Steven Greene looked as pale as death.

She went up the steps to the door and knocked. There was no sound. She called, "Hallo!" and knocked again.

Finally, there were footsteps and some words she could not make out. The door opened. The woman who stood there was big, busty, wearing the old costume, gray hair tied in a bun the way the good Catholic women of this village had always tied their hair. She had glasses on. Lee would have recognized her anywhere. The woman took her glasses off and peered at Lee's face.

"Fräulein Stein," she said, not asking, stating, in the same voice that dominated hours of tapes, told countless tales of truth and fantasy.

"Frau Möck." Lee held out her hand. "I'm sorry it took me so long to come back, but I never forgot you. I've brought someone to see you." She started back to the car but the door had already opened and Steven Greene was getting out. He closed the door, looked up at the house and housewife, and slowly made his way to her.

Frau Möck's eyes widened and filled with tears. "Simon," she said, starting down the steps. *"Simon."*

Lee turned away. She looked up the road that led into the village. Next door, a woman was sweeping her steps with her face in the direction of the walk between the Mercedes and the door to the Möck house. It was a comical sight, the woman's hands whisking away at the same spot over and over, the eyes glued to something just to Lee's left.

"Come, Fräulein Stein," a tearful voice said. "In the house."

She turned to see Steve wiping his face with a large handkerchief. He stuffed it in a pocket and squeezed Lee's hand. Together, the three of them walked into the house.

Frau Möck started calling names. She ran to the stairs and called. She went to the back door and called. She came back and said, "Sit, sit. Please sit down."

They sat at the kitchen table. The kitchen was larger, encompassing the old shed that had been attached to it. There was an electric stove against the same wall where the old wood stove had been and on another wall, a small, new-looking refrigerator.

People poured into the kitchen. One was a sister-in-law, older now, but still recognizable. A man about seventy came

277

in, hugged Steve, brushed a tear from his eye, and sat beside him, holding onto his hand with both of his, talking and smiling. Women Lee had never seen before came in, and children.

Frau Möck grabbed a little blond girl and said, "Quick, run to Gnau and tell them Simon is here. Quick!"

The little girl disappeared. Someone put a bottle of wine on the table and someone else brought two glasses. The older man opened the bottle, poured, and gave a glass to Lee and a glass to Steve.

"Please," Lee said. "You and Frau Möck must join us."

"You're right." He waved to his wife. "Two more glasses. Come and sit beside your son. Hannes," he called into the crowd, "where is your camera?"

At that moment, the little blond girl walked in the front door with a man and woman about Steve's age. The girl pointed to the kitchen and the man made his way to the table. He looked hard at Steve's face, his head nodding. He grasped Steve's hand and shook it.

"It's the same face," he said. "You see that?" he asked his mother. "The face never changed."

Somebody pushed beside Lee and started taking pictures across the table. Lee moved her chair out of the way, then stood and slipped out of the crowd. She walked out the back door, a door she had never used before, and walked to a small barn. A weathered old man with very few teeth wished her a good day and she returned the greeting. It was warm but quite breezy. She kept walking. These were the fields at the edge of town where each farming family owned its plot, grew its food, kept itself alive in the awful weeks and months after the war when there was nothing to eat because Germany could no longer ravage the farmland of France and keep the French hungry to feed the Germans. Frau Möck had never chastised her for two decades of forgetfulness. She had waited and it had happened.

I made her happy, Lee thought, walking farther and farther from the house, through fields planted in perfect rows, the way farmers always seemed to manage, without computers or calculators or modern scientific tools. And Frau Biehl has made me happy. And that's it. It goes no further. Because I don't really have the strength to end it, I will continue to see him for one day and two nights forty-some weeks of the year until we tire of it or of each other, or until he moves to California to start his new life. Or until something else gets in the way.

And I will do what I am now old enough and capable enough and independent enough to do on my own. She had stopped walking. The sun was close enough to overhead that it must be noon. Rich would be in Frankfurt now, looking at his church on Beethovenstrasse, walking through old streets.

"Fräulein Stein, Fräulein Stein!" It was a young voice, far away.

Lee turned. She had walked farther than she had thought. The house seemed like one of a row of distant little doll houses at the end of a flat plain. The little blond girl was running across the field, waving to her. She waved back.

"Are you Fräulein Stein?" the little girl asked, panting, as she arrived.

"Yes, I am."

"My grandmother says you are to come back to the house. Please," she added as an afterthought. "You didn't finish your wine."

Lee smiled. "Let's walk back together."

"Bitte schön."

She took the child's hand. "How old are you?"

279

"Seven."

"I had a little girl once. When she was seven we took a walk like this one day."

"Where is she?"

"She died."

"Oh. I'm sorry. Maybe God will give you another one."

"Maybe He will. I'd like that."

"Who is the man you brought here?"

"He's a man your grandmother was once very good to."

"My grandmother is good to everyone."

"You're right. She is." The child used the word "Oma" for grandmother. Oma had been the old woman who had peeled potatoes in the shed that no longer existed. Oma had always seemed to Lee to mean "very old woman," although Frau Biehl, who was younger and stylish, was called that by her grandsons.

They walked lazily, Lee enjoying the feel of the little hand in hers. When they reached the house, the camera pointed at her several times and the sisters-in-law asked her a million questions. And she sat at the table and dutifully finished her glass of wine.

They made it back to Frau Biehl's by four for coffee and cake. Rich was not there. Steve had had enough of crowds and foreign language and excitement and wanted only to return to his hotel room, but he acknowledged the importance of honoring Frau Biehl's invitation. She wanted the whole day recounted and she listened with genuine interest.

"Lee always said she would find you," she said when the retelling was done. "I knew she would. When you come back with your wife and children, Mr. Greene, you will stay with me. My bedrooms are never filled."

"That's very kind of you."

Rich arrived at a quarter to five and if Frau Biehl was irritated, she did not show it. The coffee was still hot, there was plenty of cake, and she went out to the kitchen to whip some fresh cream for him.

"How was it?" Lee asked.

"Different. The church isn't bad, but I miss the weeds. And the sky instead of a roof. There was no one left at my house who remembered me. The old couple have been gone for a long time."

Frau Biehl came in with the cream and he helped himself and thanked her.

"But Justice is still there at the town hall, holding her scales with her eyes wide open." He turned to Steve. "You must have had an interesting day."

"More emotional than anything I've experienced in many years," Steve said. "Too much for one day. I probably won't sleep tonight." He patted his jacket pocket. "She gave me something before we left. Let's see what it is." He pulled out a small brown envelope, folded in half. He smoothed it on his knee and pulled something out. "My God." He laid it on a napkin on the coffee table. It was a yellow star. "My God," he said again.

"Those were terrible times," Frau Biehl said. "Terrible. But they are gone now, Mr. Greene. I promise you."

"If promises were horses," Rich paraphrased, speaking English, "then beggars would ride."

"But what else is there?" Steve said. "What else can there ever be? At least we have the promise of a few good people." He leaned across the table and patted Frau Biehl's hand. "Thank you," he said in clear German. She smiled.

He put the star back in the envelope and put the envelope carefully in his inside jacket pocket. "I'm going to try to get

281

myself on a plane tomorrow, Lee," he said. "When were you planning to leave?"

She looked at Rich.

"Whenever you want," he said.

"I'd like to stay through Sunday."

"I'm sure I can drive to the airport if you direct me," Steve said. "I'll have to drive if we come back."

"Will you come back?" Lee asked.

"Oh, yes. I think my children would like to see that house. It would be nice to sit and talk quietly with the Möcks. And I'd like to visit number twenty-seven if they'll let me. Maybe in the spring, when school is out."

She gave him the car key and he said his good-byes, Frau Biehl exacting a promise that he would visit her.

When he had left, they sat quietly in the living room. Frau Biehl opened a bottle of sweet vermouth and poured three glasses.

"It's good at the end of the day," she said. "Good for the heart."

At six the phone rang. Frau Biehl answered and talked for several minutes. When she came to the living room, she motioned to Lee. "It's Martina. Speak to her."

"Martina! How are you?"

"Lee. Why didn't you tell me you were coming? We could have driven up for the weekend."

"It was a busy enough weekend for your mother. Did she tell you?"

"Everything. You must write me a long letter. I can't believe half of what she told me."

"It's all true. How are you?"

"We're fine. How do you find Mummy?"

"Wonderful."

"I don't know, Lee. Have you been to the cemetery?"

"We went this morning."

"Then you saw it. Mummy is getting old. She's starting to do things that are strange."

"Marty, what she did was wonderful. That's our Tina that's buried there, not some theoretical person named Christine."

"It doesn't seem right." Marty sounded disappointed. She had lost an ally.

"It is right."

"What else did she say?"

"Not much. We've all been doing a lot of talking."

"I wish I were there. Promise you'll visit us."

"I promise.

"And your Rich. Tell him when I was twelve, I was in love with him."

"I'll tell him."

"*Tschüss,* Lee."

"*Tschüss.*"

Chapter Seven

He picked her up on Sunday morning after breakfast and they drove out to the ruin again in the Opel.

"It's a nice spot," he said. "It's surprising so few people visit it."

"I've never seen it in a guidebook. It's sort of the town secret."

They walked inside; he touched the walls.

"Do you want to go to the cemetery?" she asked.

"It's the reason I came."

"I went yesterday morning with Frau Biehl. She used the name Tina on the stone instead of the Christian name. That's what her daughters are upset about. They think she's losing touch with reality. I'm very moved by what she did. I picked the name."

"Why don't we drive over."

She directed him back to the center of town and then, with only one wrong turn, to the cemetery. "I always feel a knot inside me when I go," she confessed.

"If it makes any difference, so do I," he said.

He parked and they started to walk. He took her hand. His felt slightly clammy, not like the dry little hand she had held yesterday on the farm.

"That's the plot," she said as it came into view, the beautiful white stone marker. Our child, she thought, as they neared it. "She was so good, Rich."

He let go her hand and put his arm around her shoulder.

They stopped in front of the stone, parents mourning their lost daughter.

"You OK?" he said.

"No." She dug for a tissue, pressed it to her eyes, slipped her arm around him. After a minute she left him and went to the trees, looking for her stone. His eyes were on her as she came back. She knelt and left the stone among the flowers.

"Are you pregnant?" he asked when she had stood.

The question took her by surprise. "I don't know," she said.

He shook his head. "Don't say things like that to me."

"It's my responsibility, Rich, not yours."

"We know each other too well for that. Have I ever shirked my responsibility?"

"No. But you made it quite clear that your plans don't include a permanent relationship."

"You haven't learned a damn thing in twenty years, have you? You still listen too much to what I say. I'm here, aren't I?"

"I gave Cal notice that I wanted to sell my share. The accountant is doing whatever accountants do to figure out what that's worth. I told him I want to take off a couple of years. It'll probably—if all goes well—I'll give birth in March. Around Tina's birthday. I'll be forty-three," she added.

"I can count. Have you specifically ruled me out of all this?"

"I've never ruled you out of anything. You know that."

He pushed her hair back from her forehead. "Do we need the help of an accountant to rule me in?"

She smiled. "No."

"Would you consider spending tonight in a posh hotel in

Frankfurt? Together. In one room. I made the reservation this morning."

"I'll consider it."

"Is there anything else we have to say? While we're here."

"Not anymore."

They turned away from the stone to go back to the car. Frau Biehl was approaching, carrying a few flowers from the garden.

Rich offered her his hand and they shook. "Thank you," he said.

"There is nothing to thank. We are a family."

"Lee and I are going to leave you this afternoon. We'll stay overnight in Frankfurt. It'll be easier to get to the airport to-morrow morning."

"A good idea," Frau Biehl said. "I was going to suggest it myself. We'll have a nice dinner, I'll go up to my bed and you'll drive to Frankfurt. A good arrangement."

"I appreciate everything you've done for Lee."

"I do nothing for her. She does everything for me. She's better to me than my daughters. After dinner," she turned to Lee, "I will give you my pearls. They're too elegant for a small town like this. They're better for New York. Or Wash-ington," she said, smiling at Rich.

Lee said, "Thank you. I'll think of you every time I wear them."

"That's good, to have someone who thinks of you. I've de-cided not to sell the house till next year."

"I'm glad," Lee said. "I can't picture you anywhere else."

"I'll need the house when Mr. Greene comes with his fam-ily. And who knows? Maybe Martina will come for Christ-mas."

"Lee is moving to Washington," Rich said.

"I am?"

"You can write to her at my address. It's on those letters I sent you."

Frau Biehl smiled. "The address is already in my book, Richard." She walked to the grave, laid the flowers in front of it, and came back. "My daughters are angry with me because I kept Tina home that last year. They think she should have had a semester at the university. I couldn't allow it." She was speaking to Rich. "She wanted to go to Munich. I couldn't let her go away. My daughters are mothers but they don't understand. I did what I thought was right."

"That's all we can ask of any person, that you do what you think right," Rich said.

"I'm glad you understand."

"Let us drive you home," Lee said.

"Thank you, but I like a walk in the morning. I'll go to the car with you. I'll be home in time for dinner." She put one arm around Rich and the other around Lee and the three of them walked to the car. "You should walk more, both of you. Driving around in a car, it's not *gesund*. You should think of the heart, the lungs. I am a doctor's wife. I know these things."

From across the cemetery, a black shadow shaped like a giant bird raced toward them, skimming the ground, absorbing the three of them, and flying away. Rich took Lee's hand. It was cool and dry. Frau Biehl looked up, her eyes searching the clear sky.

"The gliders," she said. "How he loved them." She waved to them, turned, and walked back to the stone.

Rich drove out the way they had come and stopped the car across the road from the cemetery. "Are we ready to move on now?" he asked, the motor idling as though they had somewhere to go.

"I'm ready." She placed her hand on her still-flat abdomen

287

for the first time.

"Would you mind a little detour this afternoon on the way to Frankfurt? Frau Biehl told me about a ruin, a pair of towers near Giessen."

"Do we climb or just look?"

"We do what we always do. We climb."

"I wouldn't mind at all," she said.